"You can't deny you wanted me to touch you," Rowe said.

His look made desire claw at her, tempting her anew. "I did want it, but I shouldn't have," Kirsten replied.

"Why not? Neither of us is married." His glare intensified. "You're not committed to anyone, are you? Is it Jeffrey's father?"

The truth must have been reflected in her gaze because Rowe's expression softened. "I should have thought of that before. Did he hurt you badly?"

Choosing her words with care, she said, "Jeffrey's father never loved me."

"And you didn't find out until you were pregnant?" His long fingers tightened their grip. "I would never do such a thing to you, Kirsten."

The savage intensity in his assertion made it difficult to remember that it was *exactly* what he had done to her sist

Dear Reader,

October is bringing big changes in the Silhouette and Harlequin worlds. To strengthen the terrific lineup of stories we offer, Silhouette Romance will be moving to four fabulous titles each month.

Don't miss the newest story in this six-book series— MARRYING THE BOSS'S DAUGHTER. In this second title, *Her Pregnant Agenda* (#1690) by Linda Goodnight, Emily Winters is up to her old matchmaking tricks. This time she has a bachelor lawyer and his alluring secretary—a single mom-to-be—on her matrimonial short list.

Valerie Parv launches her newest three-book miniseries, THE CARRAMER TRUST, with *The Viscount & the Virgin* (#1691). In it, an arrogant royal learns a thing or two about love from his secret son's sassy aunt. This is the third continuation of Parv's beloved Carramer saga.

An ornery M.D. is in danger of losing his heart to a sweet young nurse, in *The Most Eligible Doctor* (#1692) by reader favorite Karen Rose Smith. And is it possible to love a two-in-one cowboy? Meet the feisty teacher who does, in Doris Rangel's magical *Marlie's Mystery Man* (#1693), our latest SOULMATES title.

I encourage you to sample all four of these heartwarming romantic titles from Silhouette Romance this month.

Enjoy!

Mavis C. Allen
Associate Senior Editor, Silhouette Romance

Please address questions and book requests to:
Silhouette Reader Service
U.S.: 3010 Walden Ave., P.O. Box 1325, Buffalo, NY 14269
Canadian: P.O. Box 609, Fort Erie, Ont. L2A 5X3

The Viscount & the Virgin

VALERIE PARV

THE CARRAMER TRUST

SILHOUETTE *Romance*®

Published by Silhouette Books

America's Publisher of Contemporary Romance

To David and Judy,
Carramer citizens by right of friendship.

 SILHOUETTE BOOKS

ISBN 0-373-19691-1

THE VISCOUNT & THE VIRGIN

This edition published by arrangement with Harlequin Books S.A.

® and TM are trademarks of Harlequin Books S.A., used under license.
Trademarks indicated with ® are registered in the United States Patent
and Trademark Office, the Canadian Trade Marks Office and in other
countries.

Visit Silhouette at www.eHarlequin.com

Printed in U.S.A.

VALERIE PARV

lives and breathes romance and has even written a guide to being romantic, crediting her cartoonist husband of nearly thirty years as her inspiration. As a former buffalo and crocodile hunter in Australia's Northern Territory, he's ready-made hero material, she says.

When not writing her novels and nonfiction books, or speaking about romance on Australian radio and television, Valerie enjoys dollhouses, being a *Star Trek* fan and playing with food (in cooking that is). Valerie agrees with actor Nichelle Nichols, who said, "The difference between fantasy and fact is that fantasy simply hasn't happened yet."

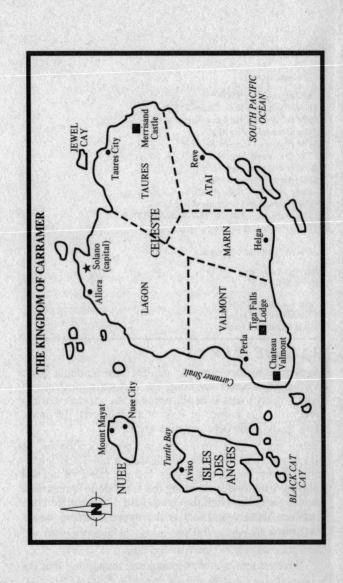

THE KINGDOM OF CARRAMER

Chapter One

Kirsten Bond took a deep breath, tried to ignore the complaints her feet were making about the new shoes she had foolishly chosen to wear, and smiled broadly at the group clustered around her. This was the last tour of the day. As soon as it ended, she would close the door of her office, kick off the shoes and reward herself with a cool drink, she promised herself. She sneaked a glance at her watch. Only fifteen minutes to go.

She resisted the urge to groan aloud. Served her right for being seduced by five-inch heels and teensy black ankle straps that the sales person had assured her made her legs look fabulous. At five foot three, she wanted all the help the heels could provide, and had bought the shoes on impulse. She should have had the sense to break them in at home before wearing them to her job at the castle, where she was on her feet for a good part of the day.

Nevertheless, she was managing, managing, that is,

until a tall, good-looking man attached himself to the
back of the group. Of itself, there was nothing wrong
with him choosing to participate. Tours of Merrisand
Castle were free and people often joined in after the
start if they'd arrived late. Normally Kirsten nodded
a welcome and kept on describing the castle and its
wonderful art treasures. The collection belonged to
the Carramer royal family, but Kirsten, as enthusiastic
as the most ardent collector, looked on the beautiful
objects almost as her own.

With the arrival of this particular newcomer, her
normally fluent spiel faltered and she felt her mouth
go dry. What was Romain Sevrin doing here? He
never came to the castle, or she wouldn't have risked
taking a job here. The last time she'd seen him on
television, he was driving ridiculously fast cars
around the racing circuits of Europe, collecting trophies at about the same rate as he collected super-
models.

The attraction wasn't hard to see. Romain, or Rowe
as he was usually called, was a little over six feet tall
with the dark coloring, brooding good looks and thick
glossy hair shared by many male members of the
royal family. The gaze he directed at her was a bril-
liant sea-green under lush dark lashes. When he
turned his head slightly, he displayed an aristocratic
profile that wouldn't have been out of place on a clas-
sical sculpture.

She, on the other hand, did not have the sort of
supermodel beauty to deserve his steady scrutiny, a
scrutiny that made her feel as if he was committing
her features to memory. Apart from being only average height, she had shoulder-length red hair shot
through with gold highlights so it looked like dancing

flames. Left to itself, it curled in all directions, so she usually wore it caught by a clasp at her nape, although a few tendrils invariably escaped to make her features look even finer-boned than they were. Large, silver-gray eyes completed a picture she would willingly have exchanged for blond hair and blue eyes any day.

According to her friends, her temper was the equal of her fiery hair although she was sure this was an exaggeration. Well, maybe she was just a little quick-tempered, but she didn't have the hair-trigger temper usually thought to go with being a redhead. If she had, she would have demanded to know what Romain Sevrin wanted.

He rarely used his title, but as Viscount Aragon, he surely had no need to tag along, listening to her describe works of art he must have grown up around. And he certainly had no need to look at her with such blatant interest. He made her feel as if she, and not her commentary, was the focus of his attention.

She shifted from one foot to the other, eliciting a fresh wave of complaint from her poor feet. This time she barely noticed. She was too busy dealing with the primitive emotions his inspection stirred within her.

Suddenly she was aware of every throbbing beat of her pulse, and the air in the baronial hall, temperature-controlled to protect the valuable contents, felt stiflingly hot. She resisted the urge to mop her brow, sure that the perception was as much a fantasy as her interpretation of his gaze. What was he doing here?

One of the visitors claimed her attention. "Does the legend apply only to members of the royal family?"

With Rowe listening intently, Kirsten wished she had left out her usual mention of the Merrisand legend. Too late now. She cleared her throat. "The legend says that anyone who serves the Merrisand Trust will be rewarded by finding true love, so it doesn't only apply to royalty."

Rowe looked distinctly interested in the subject. She avoided his eyes, recognizing another man in the group. "How large is the Merrisand estate?" the man, an American, asked.

Hoping her relief at the change of subject wasn't too obvious, she turned her attention to the questioner, although awareness of the viscount hovered at the fringe of her consciousness. She could even smell traces of his aftershave lotion, something foresty and fresh, and utterly masculine.

She really was imagining things, she told herself as she gathered her thoughts. The room they were in had thirty-foot ceilings and walls a dozen yards apart. Any lingering scent should quickly dissipate in this space.

All the same, she could smell a woodsy fragrance that hadn't been present until Rowe arrived. When he'd opened the great double doors to let himself in, the aroma had probably drifted in on the breeze from the forest surrounding the castle. Or so she tried to convince herself. It didn't explain why her every sense felt magnified in his presence.

She cleared her throat. "When the castle was built in 1879, the original estate granted to Honoré de Marigny, the first Marquis of Merrisand, consisted of about two thousand acres of hill, forest and small tenant farms. Over the years the land has been expanded to about eight thousand acres, including a sanctuary planted with trees to provide breeding grounds for the native sun deer, the faunal emblem of Carramer."

Honoré would have been Romain's great-great-grandfather, her one-track mind insisted on supplying.

The questioner nodded thoughtfully, digesting the information. A teenage girl raised her hand. "How do you get a job working in the castle?"

It was a fairly common question. "Merrisand Castle is like a city on a small scale, with career opportunities in everything from land management and animal husbandry to historical research and media. It's best to qualify in your area of interest first, then ask the controller of staff to advise you if an opening arises in your field."

"Did you always want to be a tour guide?" a resonant voice asked.

Without looking, she knew that it belonged to Rowe Sevrin. She directed her answer to the group, although her voice came out annoyingly husky. "I'm not strictly a tour guide, although like many of the staff, I conduct tours when needed. My title is art curator to the Merrisand Trust. I studied fine arts at university, majoring in the conservation of cultural materials, and interned at the castle while I was studying. When a job became available looking after the royal collections, I applied and was accepted."

"Just like that," he drawled.

She met his gaze directly this time, well aware of some cat-and-mouse game taking place. But why? And how had she become cast in the role of mouse? She decided that the best defense was offense. "Is there a problem, Viscount Aragon?"

As she had intended, her use of his title caused a stir within the group. Murmuring, they turned to regard Rowe curiously. His frown deepened, his face taking on the look of the sky before a thunderstorm.

Determinedly, she sailed on. "Ladies and gentlemen, since we have the rare privilege of having the viscount among us, perhaps you have questions you'd like to ask him. I'm sure you'll be happy to answer them, won't you, Your Lordship?

Too late and too bad if he didn't, she thought as he shot her a glare that would have melted ice. If he didn't want to be recognized, he shouldn't have joined the group and thrown her off stride. Just how he could have done so with such ease, she wasn't sure. For now she had turned the tables and he was the one on the defensive.

"I'll be delighted," he said smoothly, his honeyed tone belying his thunderous expression. The gaze he shot at her plainly said, *Later, for you.*

She swallowed hard, wondering what she had unleashed, and why she'd felt so moved to challenge him. Normally if members of the royal family appeared while she was giving a talk, she accorded them their privacy unless they made it obvious that they wished to contribute. Why had she felt the need to assert herself with him?

The members of the group had no such concerns. When the time came to end the tour, they were still besieging him with questions. One or two of the younger visitors had asked him to autograph their guide books. As Rowe Sevrin, former champion Formula One racing driver, or Viscount Aragon? she wondered. She debated whether to leave him to it, but her conscience wouldn't permit it. She already felt badly for dragging him into the spotlight. No matter how she felt about him, she had no right to subject him to such an ordeal. She resolved to tell him so as soon as the group had gone.

"I'm sure we're all grateful for the time Viscount Aragon has spent with us, but we mustn't monopolize him any longer. Some of you have transportation waiting for you at the east gate, so please join me in showing your appreciation before you leave."

Thanks to the splendid acoustics in the hall, the applause she initiated echoed for some minutes. With a smile and a salute, the viscount swung around and started to walk away. As he passed Kirsten, he said in lowered tones close to her ear, "Report to me in the curator's office as soon as you're finished here."

The summons was hardly a surprise after what she'd done, but she found it hard to keep her composure as she saw the group off. Rowe was a member of the board of the Merrisand Trust. Although he didn't attend board meetings, technically he was her superior.

He probably intended to reprimand her for drawing attention to his presence in the group, and she knew it was no more than she deserved. She had her own issues with the viscount, but they were personal, and in no way excused her unprofessional behavior.

As she returned her portable microphone and the notes she rarely needed to her office, her mind spun back to the first time she'd heard of Rowe Sevrin. She'd been an intern at the castle, struggling to master her chosen profession while trying to keep her wayward teenage sister on the straight and narrow.

Neither had been easy, but she had no notion of how badly she was failing until Natalie came home and announced that she was pregnant.

Kirsten knew Nat had been frequenting the car races at nearby Angel Falls, where a leg of the international Grand Prix was being held. Kirsten had decided her sister's interest was harmless and would wear off more quickly if she ignored it than if she made a fuss. Nat had never suggested that she was involved with anyone connected with the race.

"You'd better tell me what happened," she'd said weakly, struggling to hold back the condemnation that hovered on her lips. Since their parents' deaths two years before when Kirsten was twenty, she had feared alienating Natalie by being too bossy. Maybe if she'd laid firmer ground rules, this wouldn't have happened.

It was too late by then. Natalie had confessed that the father of her child was the racing driver Rowe Sevrin. Kirsten had been fairly sure this was non-sense. What would a sophisticated man like Sevrin, a member of the royal family, to boot, see in a teenager like Natalie?

Only by making herself see her sister objectively had Kirsten realized how oblivious she'd been. Natalie might have been young in age, but she had grown up quickly since losing their parents. She'd dressed, spoken and acted much older than her years, and had had a coquettish way that was bound to attract men.

Even Rowe Sevrin? Kirsten had finally conceded that Natalie had no reason to lie to her and so had developed a powerful anger toward the viscount for his role in the affair. Even though he couldn't have been more than twenty-two himself at the time, he should have taken more care. For although Natalie looked womanly and was legally an adult, she was still a vulnerable innocent, grieving for her parents.

Natalie had thrown a tantrum worthy of baby Jeffrey when Kirsten suggested she telephone the vis-count. "Most women would be eager to be involved with a member of the royal family,'' Kirsten had said by way of encouragement.

Natalie's response had been totally unexpected. ''Most women wouldn't have given him a false name and told him they were on the pill.''

Under Kirsten's gentle probing, Natalie had admitted that she had crashed a party to celebrate the viscount's team winning the championship. When the viscount's security people had demanded her name, she'd given them a false last name.

According to Natalie, Rowe himself had been watching the party from a shadowed terrace and had said she could stay. Intending to thank him for intervening on her behalf, she'd noticed how distressed he seemed, and they'd started talking, during which she shared with him some of her own deep unhappiness. He'd suggested she join him for dinner after the party and she had never gotten around to telling him her real name. One thing had led to another, and then she was expecting his child. He might well think, Natalie had protested, that she had pretended to be on the pill to trap him into fathering her baby.

He didn't have to like it, he only had to take his share of the responsibility, Kirsten had insisted. She felt sorry for Natalie for getting herself into such a predicament, but Rowe was entitled to be told.

Natalie sister needn't have worried. Rowe had already moved on to the next stage of the Formula One circuit and she was told he wasn't available. He probably had no wish to be bothered by a girl he had used and abandoned on the previous leg, Kirsten assumed. Her sister's calls were never returned.

Through her contacts at the castle, Kirsten had obtained a postal address for him and insisted Natalie write and tell Rowe she was expecting his child. Natalie hadn't wanted to send the letter, but Kirsten vowed that *she* would if Natalie didn't. So the letter was sent, but no reply came.

Then they'd heard that Rowe had given up racing and had established an event-management organization. With his connections, Kirsten wasn't surprised that the business was now reputed to be worth a fortune, quite apart from his royal inheritance.

She had debated whether to try to contact him again, but Natalie had stood firm this time, declaring that she wanted nothing to do with a man who ignored the birth of his own child. This time, Kirsten didn't argue.

As a parent, Natalie hadn't done much better, Kirsten thought with a wry twist of her lips. When the baby, an adorable little boy, was born, Natalie had been eager to have Kirsten take over most of his care. Natalie returned to the racing scene, making Kirsten glad that Rowe was no longer part of it, and couldn't hurt her sister with his indifference more than he already had.

Kirsten knew she should have tried to make Natalie more accountable, for Jeffrey's sake if not her own, but she hadn't had the heart. Nat had lost so much, with her parents and then being abandoned by her baby's father. Her sister had had so little time to be young that Kirsten willingly juggled her commitments so she could look after Jeffrey, telling herself that Natalie would settle down and resume her responsibilities if given enough time.

As things turned out, time was something neither of them were granted. Watching a qualifying race before a major event, Natalie had been killed when a tire flew off a car, bounced over a protective barrier and slammed into her.

Jeffrey had been six months old at the time. He was six years old now. Without him, Kirsten didn't know how she would have survived the grief of losing her sister after her parents. Having the baby to care for meant Kirsten couldn't afford to indulge her own feelings.

For Jeffrey's sake she had battled through the dark aftermath of Nat's death and had doggedly completed her studies by correspondence in time for Jeffrey's first birthday. Although he was too young to appreciate her efforts, she had baked him a cake with a huge single candle, and they had celebrated together, her pleasure shadowed by memories of loved ones who were no longer with them.

Jeffrey had become her only family, as she had become his. She was the only mother he knew. By his silence, Rowe had forfeited any right to be involved in the child's life. If he had answered Nat's letter or shown any interest in Jeffrey at all, Kirsten would have felt duty bound to share the child's upbringing with him, but he hadn't called or written. Did he even know that Natalie had a sister who was now a mother to his child in every way that mattered?

He had been retired from racing by then, but he must have read about Natalie's death, although she probably meant nothing more to him than a one-night stand, Kirsten thought, feeling choked. Her sister had written to him telling him her real name. Would he even remember her, given the number of women he was reputed to have been involved with? He hadn't shown any interest in whether the child had ever been born, much less whether he had a son or daughter.

Kirsten felt her body begin to heat with remorse. She had actually allowed herself to feel aroused by his blatant appraisal, when he was the last man she should want to have anything to do with. It couldn't be helped that he was a member of the Merrisand board, and as such, was entitled to demand her deference. She didn't have to respond as if he was a divine gift to women.

With a start, Kirsten realized that twenty minutes had passed since she'd returned to the office and become lost in her memories. She had eased the new shoes off, and her feet looked red and sore, as indeed they felt. But she had no other shoes in the office, and Rowe was probably pacing the curator's office even now. He didn't strike her as a man who appreciated being kept waiting.

Reluctantly, she put the shoes back on and got to her feet, feeling as if her toes were being jabbed with pins. She hoped Rowe would keep this meeting short so she could collect Jeffrey from the Castle School and go home. With the head curator, Lea Landon, in Europe looking after a touring exhibition of treasures from the royal collection, Kirsten was carrying most of the load. She wished that Rowe hadn't chosen today to put in his appearance.

There would never be a good time, she thought as she made her way to the curator's office. Rowe's history with her sister meant she was never likely to welcome his arrival. The sooner she got this meeting over with, the better.

Chapter Two

Rowe Sevrin wasn't pacing the office, but he was sorely tempted. His reaction to the woman Maxim had told him he would be working with had caught him completely by surprise. He was glad his royal cousin hadn't been there to see Rowe's response to Kirsten Bond, or he would never have heard the end of it.

While she was undeniably attractive, he'd dated more than his share of beautiful women in his days on the racing circuit. Rather, Kirsten had an arresting quality that was lacking in more conventionally pretty females. Maybe it was her passion for her subject, but as she talked, he'd been captivated by the way her fine-boned face lit up with a glow that couldn't be faked.

As a man of strong passions himself, he found such unbridled verve a positive turn-on. He imagined taking Kirsten out and encouraging her to share her passions with him, and found the notion more arousing than he liked. Wasn't he the one who had vowed to steer clear of romantic entanglements for the time being? Too many of the women he'd dated had coveted the title of viscountess to the point where he had begun to question whether the attraction was him or his royal status.

He gave vent to a sigh of irritation. Why didn't he admit the truth to himself? He was tired of investing his energy in relationships that went nowhere. At twenty-nine years old, he'd almost given up the notion of finding one woman with whom he could have a home, children, the whole package.

Not that he intended to remain celibate. He wasn't that far into self-denial. But for now, any relationship he embarked upon would be purely physical by mutual agreement. It was just as well that many women found such liaisons appealing for the same reasons he did. They were happy with the comfort of a physical relationship without the idea that anything more meaningful was involved, making him unlikely to want for bed partners. You never knew, he might even stumble across his soul mate that way. Sometimes the thing you most wanted came to you only when you stopped searching for it.

None of which had anything to do with Kirsten Bond. From the way she had thrown him to the wolves during the tour without even batting a long-eyelashed eye, she was hardly likely to qualify as soul-mate material, so why was he wasting time thinking about her in that way?

She intrigued him, that was why. Not only her energy, but her air of self-possession made her seem much more than a palace employee. She hadn't been awed by his title. After fending off the candidates for viscountess, he was bound to find Kirsten's indifference a challenge, but he knew that was only a minor part of her appeal. There was only one solution—get to know her better and satisfy himself that he was seeing more in her than she warranted.

On the curator's desk was a state-of-the-art laptop computer. Rowe pulled it toward him and called up the castle's personnel records. Keying in his password got him swiftly past the security screens and he was soon looking at Kirsten's photo and employment record.

Sweet was how she looked, he thought, letting his gaze linger on the picture. When this was taken, her hair had been shorter, fluffing around her head like a fiery halo. She looked pure and innocent, untouched by the ways of the wicked world, the very opposite of the kind of women he was used to dating. Was that the source of the appeal he could feel coiling through him as he studied her image?

He scrolled through her record, his hand freezing over a line that indicated she had a six-year-old child. A spear of disappointment shafted through him at the discovery that she was probably married. Why hadn't he thought of that? According to this, she was twenty-seven years old. He should have expected a woman as attractive as she was to be spoken for by now.

He steeled himself to find mention of a husband, not sure he liked the urge to do violence that had gripped him without warning. He should be glad if Kirsten was married. It would save him the trouble of deciding how she might fit into his life.

His spirits took an unwarranted jolt upward again as he read that her marital status was single. Not widowed. And not divorced. Like him, she was from Carramer, where divorce had never been legalized. So she was a single mother. He sat back and stroked his chin with thumb and index finger, trying to analyze his confused feelings. When he thought she might be married, he had itched to get his hands around her husband's neck. Now that he knew she was single and not the innocent he'd seemed, how did he feel?

He let a slow grin spread across his features as he answered his own question. He felt foolishly pleased, that was how. She was single, therefore available. And she had a child, so he was unlikely to raise her hope of something permanent by pursuing her. All he needed was for her to feel the same way he did, and if he couldn't convince her, he wasn't the man he thought he was.

A knock at the office door interrupted his thoughts. He flicked off the computer barely in time to stop Kirsten seeing her own face on the screen as she entered without waiting for his response.

Her gaze flickered from the computer and back to him, making him wonder if she'd glimpsed the document, after all. Her composed expression gave him no clues. A challenge indeed, this Kirsten Bond.

Had Rowe Sevrin really been studying her file? Kirsten asked herself as she took the seat he indicated across the desk from him. He'd switched the computer off as she came in, but she could have sworn he'd been looking at her picture.

The interested look he turned on her now suggested she was right. But why? Unless… A cold fist of apprehension gripped her heart. Unless he had discovered who she was and decided at long last to claim his son.

It wouldn't be so easy, she told herself firmly. Soon after Jeffrey was born, Natalie had drawn up a will—one of the few responsible things she had done for her child—naming Kirsten as his guardian in the event of anything happening to her. Rowe could only come between them by challenging her guardianship in a court of law.

The prospect sent a chill through Kirsten. She was careful with her money and had no real worries about everyday expenses, but a drawn-out legal battle could drain anyone's resources. Any ordinary person, that is. With his royal connections and personal fortune, Rowe was far from ordinary.

Not in any respect, her inner voice insisted. The reaction she'd had to him during the tour threatened to overwhelm her anew until she quelled it determinedly. She couldn't do much about her susceptibility to his physical attractions, but her own family history, quite apart from Rowe's role in her sister's life, should be enough to warn her away from a man like him.

Self-centered, footloose, fickle when it came to women. Mentally she ticked off Rowe's well-publicized attributes and compared them with her father's. Felix Bond, an artist, had also possessed good looks and abundant charm, qualities he had frequently employed in the pursuit of younger women. At first Kirsten thought her mother had tolerated his affairs because of her and Natalie, but that didn't explain why she stayed with him once her daughters were well into their teens. Surely she hadn't believed Felix when he swore that she was the only woman he really loved?

It was possible. Felix always could charm the birds

from the trees. For years Kirsten herself had believed her father's paintings were ahead of their time, agreeing that he couldn't possibly waste his talents working at a menial job. The scales had fallen from her eyes when, at sixteen, she'd been expected to leave school and take a job. Her dream of becoming a writer had crumbled before the need to help support her family.

She had been lucky to be hired as a receptionist for an auction house specializing in fine arts, and the idea of a career as a curator had been born. Her boss had encouraged her to return to school in the evenings and had allowed her to study the works coming up for auction.

Her plan to move into her own place had been frustrated because her mother insisted she couldn't manage without her, so Kirsten was still living at home the afternoon a violent thunderstorm was brewing. Her father had wanted her mother to drive him to a gallery some miles away to enter one of his paintings in a contest that was about to close. Her mother hadn't wanted to go, Kirsten recalled. But as usual, her father got his way, and the two of them went. On the drive home, a tree uprooted by the storm fell on their car, leaving Kirsten and Natalie on their own with no relatives in the world.

After her parents died, the experience at the gallery had enabled her to enter university as a mature student and establish herself in the art world as a curator. She didn't need another man like her father complicating her life.

The reminder didn't stop her pulse from beating ridiculously fast when Rowe turned the full brunt of his dazzling smile on her. That he was smiling struck her as odd, considering how she had singled him out during the tour. "I owe you an apology," he said.

Surprise brought her head up. "You do?"

"I shouldn't have joined your group without warning. My arrival obviously threw you off."

In ways you can't imagine, she thought. "No harm done," she said more calmly than she felt. "The visitors enjoyed meeting a real live royal."

"As much as you enjoyed seeing me get my comeuppance?"

"It wasn't personal, Your Lordship," she insisted.

He lowered long lashes over glittering eyes. "Wasn't it? When I arrived, you gave me the distinct feeling that you'd have been happier to see Jack the Ripper."

Since she couldn't argue the truth of this, she linked her hands in her lap and looked down at them. "This is the first time we've met. I really know very little about you." All of which was true. Unable to resist, she lifted her head and met his gaze full on. "You could *be* Jack the Ripper for all I know."

To her amazement, he threw back his head and laughed, the warm sound of it rolling over her like a caress. "You're a breath of fresh air, Kirsten," he said at last. "I know very little about you, too, but I already know I want you."

Kirsten felt herself blush. She'd never been so blatantly propositioned in her life. Other women might fall into his arms because of his royal status, but she didn't intend to be one of them. "Whatever you think you know about me, I assure you you're wrong," she snapped.

If she had expected him to be cowed by her response, she was disappointed. He looked infuriatingly amused as he raised a dark eyebrow. "Really? Then those come-hither looks you were giving me during the tour are part of your normal repertoire?"

"I was not giving you come-hither looks." She hadn't, had she? Then she saw the upward tilt of his mouth and realized he was teasing her.

"What you gave me was the gift of your passion, your enthusiasm for the castle and its treasures," he said on a soft outpouring of breath. "That's what I want from you, Kirsten."

Confusion made her brain freeze. "I'm not sure...I don't..."

"Relax," he said. "We both seem to have gotten off on the wrong foot. Me for thinking I should reacquaint myself with the castle through listening to your talk, and you for getting the wrong idea about my interest in you. Can we start over?"

She didn't know why they needed to, but she nodded. "As you wish, Your Lordship."

He frowned. "You can begin by dropping the title. My name is Rowe."

Did he suspect her use of his title was a deliberate attempt to keep some distance between them? Since he wasn't going to permit it, she said, "Very well, Rowe."

He nodded in satisfaction. "From your reaction, I assume that Max hasn't told you why I'm here?"

Rowe was referring to his cousin, Prince Maxim, who held the joint positions of keeper of the castle, and administrator of the Merrisand Trust, the castle's charitable arm. "The prince probably intended to tell me at our weekly meeting, which isn't until tomorrow," she said. "I'm filling in for my boss, Lea Landon."

"Who is in Europe touring with the collection," Rowe said, evidently well informed. "No wonder you found my arrival so off-putting. You didn't know I would be taking over her office until she returns."

Kirsten felt the beginnings of a headache gather behind her eyes. "You're to be the head curator in Lea's absence?"

He gave a self-deprecating grin. "That will be the day. You could write what I know about the Merrisand collection on the head of a pin."

She seriously doubted that was true, but she felt relieved that he wasn't to be her boss even temporarily. Some aggravations she just didn't need. "I'm still not sure where I fit in."

He leaned forward and linked his hands on the leather blotter protecting the antique desk. "My company specializes in event management. Big events."

"Like the Winter Olympics," she said, wanting him to know she wasn't entirely unaware of his background, either. He would be surprised at just how much she knew about him, she thought, none of it commendable.

He nodded. "Exactly. Max thinks the castle needs a big event to stimulate income for the Merrisand Trust."

She let her astonishment show on her face. "I thought the trust was doing well."

"It needs to do better. In today's world the demand for help from organizations like Merrisand is growing all the time. The income from visitors to the castle and grounds, holding fund-raisers here and sending the collections on tour are not really adequate for the increasing demands being made on the funds. If a new source of income isn't found soon, the trust may eventually have to cut back on distributions.''

The thought that Merrisand might one day have to turn away people in need was alarming. She had always assumed that the castle generated more than enough income to meet its charitable aims. Finding out that one day it might not came as a shock.

''I had no idea,'' she said.

He gave her a sharp look. ''Nobody does, so keep this information to yourself. However ironic it may be, people are more inclined to support an organization they perceive as doing well.''

'''Nothing succeeds like success,''' she quoted.

He inclined his head in agreement. ''Precisely. Besides, the castle is hardly on its last legs. Max is merely being shrewd, anticipating future demands.''

''What does he have in mind for this event?'' she asked. She couldn't imagine what else they might do that they weren't already doing to generate income.

''Max left the decision up to me. What I'm planning is an international cycling race, the Tour de Merrisand, around the castle grounds. The television rights alone will generate millions for the trust.''

The image of a horde of cyclists tearing around, and probably sometimes through, the beautiful, manicured gardens made her shudder. But not as much as another image that jumped into her mind, that of her vibrant young sister cheering on the sidelines of a Formula One race and being cut down by a runaway wheel. Kirsten wanted nothing to do with that part of his life. ''You can't be serious,'' she said, her voice husky with emotion.

His direct gaze bored into her. ''Never more so.

Why? Do you have a problem with linking the castle to a sporting event?''

She had much more than a problem with it. The very thought made her feel ill. ''I can't believe Prince Maxim would sanction such desecration,'' she said tautly.

''It isn't as if I intend to bulldoze century-old buildings in order to lay out a cycling track,'' he said, not sounding in the least fazed by her reaction. ''The race will run between the buildings and through the forest areas. Afterward, everything will be restored to exactly as it was before the event. They hold these races through the center of Rome, past the Colosseum, and nobody considers it heresy.''

She got to her feet, the sudden pain shooting up her calves reminding her of the shoes she'd managed to forget momentarily. ''Since your plans are evidently already established, I don't see why you need me at all.''

''You're going to help me make the Tour de Merrisand a reality.''

''I'm an art curator, not a…'' She had been about to say ''sports groupie,'' but the link with Natalie was too painful. ''I don't know anything about cycling,'' she finished. Probably the reason why Prince Maxim wanted Rowe to work with her, she thought.

''But you do know the castle inside and out, better than anyone else barring Lea Landon, who won't be back for some months.''

''All the more reason why I can't be spared from covering for Lea.''

Rowe stood up, too, moving around Lea's desk like a big cat newly turned loose from its cage. Even wearing the wretched high heels, Kirsten was considerably shorter than Rowe and had to tilt her head back to look up at him as he loomed closer. "I'm not calling for volunteers," he said in a low voice.

"You mean if I don't help you with the race, I'm out of a job?" She let her tone reflect her disbelief.

"You said it. I didn't."

He was every bit as self-centered as she'd read, she thought furiously. He had made up his mind that she was to assist him, and it didn't appear she was to have any say in the matter. "Who will manage the galleries, plan the new exhibitions and supervise the daily tours?" she asked.

"According to Max, you have a capable team who can share some of the load. I'm sure there's no need for you to lead tour groups personally."

"I happen to like leading the tours. They keep me in touch with how people react to the exhibits, helping me with future planning."

"Then don't give them up. Delegate some of the other tasks that you find less enjoyable."

His closeness undermined her determination to dislike him and everything he stood for. As well, she wanted to hate the very idea of a bunch of cyclists speeding through the beautiful grounds of the castle, and part of her did. But the logical side argued that he was right. If a new source of income wasn't found, the Merrisand Trust might soon have to start turning away people in need, contradicting its very reason for existence.

It wasn't because she wanted to work with Rowe, she reasoned. She couldn't deny the chemistry flaring between them, but surely she had enough incentive to deal with it in a mature, sensible way that didn't involve giving in to the attraction. She gave a stiff nod of her head. "It seems I have no choice but to go along with your plans."

"No choice at all."

He suddenly moved even closer, his gaze warm on her equally heated face. Less than a hand span of distance separated them, and for one wild, giddy moment, she wondered if he meant to kiss her. How would she respond if he did? She liked to think she would slap his handsome face, making it clear how little time she had for a man like him. Another part of her insisted on imagining the touch of his lips on hers, the teasing of tongue to tongue in a sinuous dance that set up answering shivers all the way to the core of her being.

Without warning he lifted her hand and brought it to his lips, his eyes never leaving her face. His dark gaze seemed to look deep inside her, until she wondered if he sensed her contrary thoughts.

A scorching sensation almost had her pulling her hand away until she realized it was entirely in her mind. Rowe had done no more than kiss the back of her hand in a courtly gesture such as she had seen the royal men do on many occasions. There was no call for her body to respond as if he had actually kissed her on the lips. He wasn't likely to, and she wouldn't permit it in any case. Would she?

"I'm glad we've reached an agreement," he said, releasing her hand with what she swore was reluctance.

The move was probably as calculated as the kiss itself, she told herself, striving to still the fluttering of her heart. She might have no choice about working with him, but she could choose not to respond to such

blatant gestures. Be cool and aloof. Let him know she
wasn't impressed by his practiced gallantry.

Something told her it was going to be a difficult
resolution to keep, although keep it she must. By his
treatment of her sister, Rowe had proved to be as self-
centered and unreliable as her father, Kirsten reminded herself. Thinking of him in any other way was
playing with fire.

Chapter Three

"I wish I could say you're welcome," she said stiffly, her senses returning.

His glittering gaze mocked her. "But you still think I'm a cultural vandal."

She took satisfaction in throwing his own words back at him. "You said it. I didn't."

"Touché. While we're working together, I will hold you responsible for civilizing me," he said. "You can teach me about the collections, and the history of the castle."

She'd been hoping they wouldn't see enough of each other for that. "Didn't you study those things when you were growing up here?" she asked.

His expression darkened. "I didn't grow up here."

In her head she conjured up an image of the de Marigny family tree. Rowe's grandmother had been sister to the grandfather of Carramer's present monarch. "As the son of Angelique and James, surely—"

"If you know my family's history that well, then

you know that I was eight when my father went scuba diving and never returned.''

She did know the tragic story. To this day, people speculated that the previous Viscount Aragon, James Sevrin, was still alive somewhere, perhaps living abroad after spying for another country. She didn't believe any of the fanciful explanations. More likely, he had been carried out to sea by one of the notorious riptides off Carramer's beaches. ''It was a terrible tragedy,'' she murmured.

He cocked an eyebrow at her. ''Not an international conspiracy?''

''I don't believe so.''

''Then you're in the minority. After my father disappeared, my mother took me to live at one of the royal estates in Valmont province. She made sure I had a suitably royal education there, but she never wanted to return to the castle. She hoped to escape the rumors about my father, although they followed us even to Valmont.''

Having had her share of family tragedy, Kirsten knew only too well how hard it was to deal with the loss of loved ones, and she hadn't had to cope with sensational headlines and sidelong looks from people who thought they knew the truth.

''I'm sorry,'' she said.

''You sound almost sincere.''

She bristled at the doubt she heard in his tone. ''Believe it or not, I am. I've also lost people I care about, and it's never easy, no matter who you are, or what the circumstances.''

''No.'' He half turned away, exposing his impressive profile.

He may not have grown up in the castle, but his

birthright was there in his every move, she thought. His bearing, his manner, his speech, all bespoke a self-assurance that few people possessed. "I would have thought Merrisand Castle was the last place you would want to return to," she said.

"As Rowe Sevrin, I can live with it. Max and his family were incredibly supportive when my father disappeared. Helping them is the least I can do to repay him."

She wanted to ask if he could shed his personal history as easily as his title, but decided it was none of her business. Nor had she any interest in his problems. He had done more to hurt her family than he knew, and she couldn't forgive him for it. She didn't want to feel compassion for him, and it bothered her to find her basic sense of decency at odds with her antipathy toward him.

He wasn't going to be an easy man to hate.

"I'd like to go over my plans for the race with you over dinner," he said, startling her.

Picturing herself seated across a table from him, the subdued lighting playing on his aristocratic features, she felt heat suffuse her. She felt foolishly tempted to accept, in spite of all the reasons she shouldn't. What would it like to be the focus of his attention, to feel the touch of his hand on hers across the table as he made some point, maybe to dance with him after dinner, his body aligned with hers as they moved to the music?

Stop it, she ordered herself. If they were to work together, she had to remember who and what he was, and the threat he represented if he should discover his relationship to her son. Thinking of Jeffrey strengthened her resolve. "Thank you for the invitation, but I'm not free tonight."

Interest gleamed in his flinty gaze. "Another date?"

Tempted to remind him that her private life was none of his concern, she said, instead, "A family commitment."

"Ah, yes, your son."

She'd been right—he had been reading her file. How else would he know she had a child? "I have to collect Jeffrey from school in ten minutes."

He picked up a file from the desk and tucked it under his arm. "I'll walk with you."

Having him meet Jeffrey was the last thing she wanted. "My workday finished half an hour ago," she reminded him.

He seemed unperturbed as he held the office door open for her. "Mine, too. I'm staying in the state apartments, so the school is on my way."

To go through the door she had to brush past him. As she did so, a force like electricity crackled through her, sensitizing her nerves to an alarming degree. Despair quickly followed. How could she work with him and remain aloof when he had such a disturbing effect on her?

It seemed she had no option but to let him accompany her. She could hardly deny him the freedom of the castle grounds when he had more right to them than she did. Perhaps she could convince him not to wait when they reached the school.

She had no more luck with that than with denying his powerful impact on her, she found when they reached the building housing the school for the children of castle employees. Once a hunting lodge, the late-nineteenth-century building was as large as many mansions. Built of creamy Carramer sandstone, it was two stories high with mullioned windows, heavy timber doors and ornate wrought-iron gates. A garden of fragrant rambler roses edged a large swath of lush green lawn where children played. One fenced-off area was reserved for the smaller children, and it was here she often found Jeffrey playing with his toy cars in the sandpit. The playground was empty today, the children still inside.

"I mustn't keep you," she said by way of a hint to Rowe that it was time for him to leave.

He angled his shoulder against the stone wall of the building. "I'm in no hurry. I remember this place."

"You went to school here?"

He nodded. "Until I was seven. I missed a lot of the next year because of the turmoil surrounding my father's disappearance. After we moved, I was provided with tutors, then I attended school and university in Valmont. They were admirable places of learning, but never had the atmosphere I remember from the Castle School."

She thought the same and considered herself fortunate to be able to enroll Jeffrey in such a wonderful place, one of the key reasons she was determined not to jeopardize her position at the castle. Did Rowe suspect that when he threatened her job in order to gain her cooperation?

A fresh wave of anger toward him swamped some of the attraction. Whatever his effect on her, she should remember that he wasn't above using blackmail to get his way. "You must have more pressing things to do than wait for a group of schoolkids,'' she said pointedly.

"Undoubtedly, but they can wait. I want to meet your son."

Fear shrilled through her like a fire alarm. She didn't want him to meet Jeffrey. Rowe had no idea of his relationship to the child. If he remembered Natalie's letter at all, he wouldn't necessarily connect Natalie with Kirsten. Bond wasn't an uncommon surname. As far as he knew, Jeffrey was Kirsten's son. As long as she kept it that way, she and her child were safe.

She didn't feel safe at all.

Other parents drifted up to collect their children. Many greeted her warmly, although they left her alone in deference to the man beside her. She was aware of their speculative glances at Rowe and their murmurs of recognition. The automatic preening gestures from the women, touching their hair and smoothing their dresses, weren't lost on her, either.

She resisted the urge to feel proud of having Rowe at her side, but it was hard when he was obviously making such an impression on the other mothers. Occasionally she had wished for a more conventional family structure, for Jeffrey's sake if not her own, and Rowe's presence gave her more of a taste of what it would be like than she wanted.

He could never be part of that structure, she told herself firmly. She would work with him because she must, but to think of him as anything but her temporary boss was courting disaster.

The doors of the school swung open and a group of six-year-olds surged through, marshaled by their teacher. Among them, Kirsten spotted Jeffrey with his best friend, Michael, a red-haired terror whose father was head groundsman at the castle.

Jeffrey looked up and saw her, his small face lighting with pleasure. She felt an answering rush inside her, filling her with such love for him that she could barely restrain herself from pushing through the crowd of children and grabbing him up in a hug. She knew he considered himself a big boy now and wouldn't thank her for being what he called smoochy in front of his school friends.

Seeing the maternal pride and love on Kirsten's face as the children appeared, Rowe felt a stirring of jealousy. When he had attended school here, he had been collected by a nanny; his mother hadn't collected him until the day his father vanished, and her appearance at the school was indelibly connected with tragedy in his mind. These days the unexpected appearance of his mother still sparked a twinge of anxiety in him, until he assured himself that nothing was wrong.

Kirsten's son apparently had no such problem. From the way the little red-haired boy and his darker-haired companion made a beeline for her, the child was eager to be with her.

Before they reached her, the redhead peeled off and threw himself into the arms of a man in castle uniform waiting on the sidelines, proudly thrusting a paper kite under the man's nose. "Daddy, Daddy! Look what I made."

The dark-haired child came to Kirsten, also trailing an object made of brightly colored paper. "I made a kite, too, Mommy. We flew them in the garden today. Mine flew the best."

"I'm sure it did, sweetheart." Crouching down, Kirsten enveloped the boy in a hug, her eyes gleaming.

Rowe watched them, feeling a frown furrow his brow. His glance went from the red-haired child chattering to the man he called Daddy and back to Kirsten. Her son had inherited none of her bright coloring, but there was no mistaking the bond between them.

He suppressed a smile as he saw Jeffrey squirm out of his mother's arms. He was at the age when being cuddled in public was embarrassing. He had felt the same at that age, Rowe thought. Releasing Jeffrey with a wry expression, Kirsten stood up.

Only then did she seem to remember Rowe's presence. Color flooded her face and she took the child's hand in what looked to Rowe like a protective gesture. He didn't like the way he felt left out. He and Kirsten might not have gotten off to the best start, but he had tried to smooth things over. What more did she want?

"Jeffrey, say hello to Viscount Aragon. Rowe, this is Jeffrey," she said. He got the feeling she would have preferred not to make the introduction.

"Hello, Viscount Aragon," Jeffrey repeated dutifully. Being the kind of school it was, the children were taught early how to behave around royalty.

"Hello, son," he said. He dropped to the child's level and met huge, dark eyes that struck him as familiar somehow. Probably because Jeffrey looked a lot like himself at the same age. Same lustrous dark hair falling over his eyes. As a boy, Rowe had been forever brushing his hair out his eyes. For a meeting with the monarch when he was five, his nanny had even used her hairspray on it in desperation, he recalled with an inward shudder.

He offered his hand and the little boy shook it solemnly, the comparative size of their hands giving Rowe a strange sensation. This was how a son of his would look if he had one. In fact... He dismissed the thought out of hand. Kirsten's record didn't name her child's father, but Rowe knew without a shadow of doubt that if they had ever gone to bed together, the occasion would be burned into his memory.

Kirsten wasn't the kind of woman you made love to, then forgot about. He wondered if some man had done just that, or if Kirsten had made the choice of single parenthood herself. Either way, Rowe knew if Jeffrey had been his son, he would never have walked away, no matter what.

"Mind if I take a look at your kite?"

Jeffrey glanced at his mother for reassurance. She nodded and Jeffrey held out the mangled paper object. "Miss Sims put the string on, because we're not s'posed to use the stapler yet, but I did the rest," he explained.

Rowe restrained the smile he felt tugging at his mouth. "You can't be too careful with staplers," he agreed. "I got a staple in my thumb once."

Jeffrey looked fascinated. "Did it hurt?"

"Like you wouldn't believe, and there was lots of blood. I didn't make a fuss, though."

No, he wouldn't, Kirsten thought, hovering nearby. One quality she suspected Jeffrey had inherited from Rowe was the desire to keep his feelings concealed.

Now where had that idea come from? She barely knew the man, except through her sister's experience. She didn't want to concern herself with his feelings or, worse, see signs of him in Jeffrey. Jeffrey was her child, hers alone. Watching them together as Rowe admired the kite, she couldn't help wondering for how much longer.

"I have to get Jeffrey home," she said, unable to watch them together a moment longer. She hadn't expected to feel guilty for keeping them apart, especially since the decision had been Rowe's to begin with, but they looked so much alike that guilt assailed her now.

Jeffrey seemed fascinated with the viscount. She was horrified to hear Rowe say, "This is too good a kite to live in a cupboard. How would you like to fly it in the park sometime?"

The little boy's face shone. "Can we, Mommy?"

Furious with Rowe for putting her into such an awkward position, she said, "Viscount Aragon is a busy man, sweetheart. I'm sure he has more important things to do than fly kites. You and I will do it on our own."

Jeffrey's face crumpled. "You don't know how to fly a kite. 'Member the time you smashed my airplane?"

She remembered only too well. Last Christmas Santa Claus had visited the Castle School and had given a model plane to Jeffrey. She had painstakingly glued the model together, frustrated to find she had several bits left over afterward. Jeffrey hadn't cared. His eagerness to see the plane fly had lasted only as long as it took Kirsten to crash it into a bush a dozen feet from the launching site. One of the missing pieces had turned out to be the ballast that kept the plane on an even keel.

"This time I'll let you fly the kite," she promised.

"Why can't Viscount Aragon fly it with me?" He turned to Rowe. "You're not too busy, are you?"

Rowe gave her a searching look. "If I was, I'd have said so. But Mommy is the boss in these matters. She can tell me her decision later at the office. We're going to be working together a lot," he said for the little boy's benefit. "If she says yes, we'll go kite flying next Saturday."

Jeffrey nodded eagerly. "I'll be really good till Saturday, promise."

"Till Saturday then."

Kirsten kept her anguish from showing as she tucked her son's hand in hers, ignoring the tug that told her he'd prefer to walk by himself. She needed to feel his hand in hers to reassure herself that he was fascinated only because Rowe was a man. The Castle School had some male teachers and Jeffrey had contact with the other children's fathers, but he had no male role model at home.

And whose fault is that? she asked herself angrily, the pain in every step reminding her of the too-tight shoes. Rowe could have been involved in Jeffrey's life from the beginning. He had been the one to ignore Natalie's letter, not caring, it seemed, how the child turned out. He couldn't come along now and simply take over. She wouldn't let him.

Unaware of her fury, Rowe was continuing to walk with them. "Don't you have a home to go to?" she demanded, not caring how rude she sounded.

"My home is in Solano, the capital city of Carramer," he explained for Jeffrey's sake, adding, "Not that I've spent much time there up to now."

"You prefer to be free, I suppose." Just like her father. As a free spirit, Felix hadn't wanted to be tied down, either. Her family had lived in a series of rented houses as their father moved from one short-lived job to another. When their parents died, there had been no family home they could retreat to while they dealt with their grief. No inheritance for Jeffrey, either, making Kirsten determined to give him the most secure childhood she could, with none of the anxiety that had plagued her and Natalie while they were growing up.

Even if it meant putting up with Rowe's presence in her life until his cycling race was over, she would do it for Jeffrey's sake. Moving him from home to home was not going to happen if she could prevent it. One day she intended to buy them a place of their own. For now, they were happy here, and she would not allow Rowe's arrival to interfere.

Chapter Four

Key members of the castle staff were housed in pretty stone retainers' cottages arranged around a village green where the children often played while their parents socialized over coffee. Although the houses looked to be hundreds of years old, in reality, they had been built by the previous Marquis of Merrisand so that he could have his staff on call in case he needed them. Direct lines still connected each of the cottages with the castle switchboard.

Built on an area once known as The Tennis Courts, each cottage had its own vegetable and flower gardens, and backed onto a stand of woodland. Ring-necked partridges, quails, doves and wild turkeys frequented the woodland, attracted by Angel Creek, which crossed a corner of the castle grounds. It was an idyllic place for children, and at night Kirsten liked to pretend that the cottage and the lovely surroundings were hers alone.

"Which cottage is yours?" Rowe asked, signaling his intention to accompany her all the way home.

She gestured vaguely. "The one with the blue curtains on the other side of the green. Really, there's no need."

"It hasn't escaped my notice that you're limping," he said quietly. "I want to see that you get home in one piece."

She didn't need or welcome his concern. "I'm fine, really."

"So I can see. How did you hurt your foot?"

She was forced to be honest. "New shoes."

He frowned. "Why do women do that to themselves?"

So we have a fighting chance of meeting men like you eye to eye, she thought savagely. But it would take more than five-inch heels to achieve that miracle. And without them, Kirsten suspected she would strain her neck trying to look him in the eye.

Crossing the spongy grass, she finally admitted defeat and slipped the shoes off, hooking the straps over her fingers. Immediately she felt like a child beside Rowe. Jeffrey looked at her anxiously. "My shoes weren't very comfortable," she told him.

"Poor Mommy. You can have my turtle stool when we get home."

The stool was one of his favorite possessions, being the only one that was exactly the right height for playing computer games. She ruffled his hair. "And how will you be able to beat Michael at Doom Planet?"

Jeffrey lifted narrow shoulders. "We'll think of something."

In spite of the pain, she felt a smile start. The phrase was one she often used with Jeffrey, and it was funny to hear him use it with her. "I'm sure we will," she said, making an effort to keep a straight face.

She was achingly conscious of Rowe looming over her as she unlocked her front door. As soon as she got it open, Jeffrey scampered inside. On the threshold, she turned to Rowe. "I'll see you at the office tomorrow."

A man like Rowe was not so easily dismissed. "You heard your son. We have to think of something for your injured feet."

She didn't want Rowe ministering to her. She didn't want him in her home. "They're not injured, and I have the offer of a turtle stool," she reminded him.

"An offer that could cost your son a Doom Planet title," he rejoined. "I have no idea what Doom Planet might be, but losing sounds hazardous."

"You get turned into Jell-O or something."

Rowe's eyebrows lifted. "You'd put your son through that rather than let me help?"

"Both he and his friend, Michael, have been turned to Jell-O dozens of times and they always bounce back."

"All the same, I can suggest an alternative."

She hated to think what it might be. "Thanks, but I'm fine."

"You're turning down a massage by an expert," he warned her. "In car racing, foot and leg problems are an occupational hazard. I know some great ways to deal with sore feet."

Against all odds, she felt herself weaken. The prospect of a foot massage sounded heavenly. "Maybe for a few minutes."

"Good. I'd hate to think your suffering might put you out of action when we have so much work ahead of us."

Tension gripped her. She might have known he would have a selfish reason for wanting to help her. She began to wish she'd stayed with Jeffrey's offer of the turtle stool, but it was too late. Rowe was already following her into the house.

"Nice place," he said, looking around.

The front door opened straight into a living room she normally considered spacious. With Rowe standing in the room, the ceiling seemed lower suddenly, the walls closer.

Perfectly at ease, he scanned the small decorative touches that made the cottage home. Normally that included family photos, two of Natalie among them, but by a fluke of timing, Kirsten was having them reframed. So she didn't have to worry about Rowe recognizing Natalie's picture. Her careful arrangement of Carramer orchids and ferns could hardly compare with the armfuls of fresh flowers delivered to the castle every day, but Rowe sniffed them in evident appreciation.

"Considering how many of the world's orchids have no perfume, it's astonishing that so many of the Carramer variety smell so glorious."

She crossed her arms, then uncrossed them, not wanting to appear defensive. Exactly what he made her feel defensive about, she refused to consider. "I haven't given it much thought."

His slightly reproving gaze told her she should. "When I was traveling the Formula One circuit, I missed the scent of orchids. Like so many things we see every day yet fail to fully notice, I didn't appreciate it until it wasn't there.''

What could she say when his observation touched her on a level he couldn't possibly have intended? That she felt exactly the same way about her family? She now regretted every opportunity she'd passed up to show her sister how much she loved her, and now it was too late. Her parents had been far from perfect, too, but they had been her family, and their loss would always be with her.

''I'd better check on Jeffrey,'' she said, needing to escape the disturbing thoughts Rowe put into her mind.

He glanced through a double doorway to where he could see Jeffrey already seated at a computer. ''Is that Doom Planet I hear?''

As soon as he got through the door, the child had turned on the computer in the family room. Normally she insisted that they spend some time together outdoors before he played computer games, but today she knew she wasn't up to going out again. ''Sounds like it,'' she conceded.

The doorbell rang although the door was still ajar. ''Come in, Michael. Jeffrey's in the other room,'' she said to the red-haired child who was already halfway to that destination.

''That, I take it, is Michael,'' Rowe said.

She nodded. ''He's the son of the head groundsman, Paul Dare, and his wife, Shara, who live next door. He and Jeffrey are best friends. I'd better get them some milk and a snack. Once they turn on that computer, they'd starve to death before taking their eyes off it.''

Rowe stepped into her path. "I'll do it while you sit down. You look as if every step is agony."

It wasn't far from the truth. She wished she had the strength to argue with him. Taking care of Jeffrey was her job, and letting Rowe have anything to do with her son gave him too much chance to put two and two together. She tried to push past him, but she stumbled, unable to restrain a cry of distress.

Rowe steered her to the nearest armchair. "Sit," he ordered. "This will only take a few seconds, then it will be your turn. Where do I find the snacks?"

She gestured toward the kitchen, furious with herself for letting this happen. If she'd been more sensible in her choice of footwear, she wouldn't be in this predicament. "There's milk in the refrigerator, plastic glasses on the shelf above it and home-baked cookies in the teddy-bear jar beside them."

"Home-baked, huh? I don't suppose big boys qualify for milk and cookies, do they?"

This was getting way too cozy for comfort, but she could hardly refuse. "Help yourself."

Listening to him move around her kitchen, she had to admit it felt good to be able to relax for a few minutes and have someone else take care of things. One drawback with being a single parent was having to be on call for everything, with no one else to share the chores and worries.

Today was a one-off, she reminded herself, her eyes snapping open as they began to drift shut. She had chosen her life and she wouldn't have it any other way as long as she could be a mother to Jeffrey. She didn't need anyone else, and she especially didn't need Rowe Sevrin.

By the time Rowe had distributed the milk and cookies to the boys, then been introduced to the finer points of Doom Planet, a good twenty minutes had passed. After consulting Jeffrey about how his mother liked her coffee, Rowe made two cups, balanced cookies in the saucers and headed back to the living room.

In the doorway, he stopped in his tracks.

Kirsten was asleep in the chair.

He moved quietly into the room and set the cups carefully on a side table, then glanced around, locating a leather-covered footstool under the coffee table. He pulled it out. When he eased her feet onto it, Kirsten didn't stir, only settled herself more comfortably.

He dropped into the chair opposite her and picked up his coffee, but didn't drink. Kirsten looked like his mental picture of Sleeping Beauty. How would she react if he kissed her awake?

He frowned. Kirsten had already made it clear she didn't like him. Why not? he wondered. He wasn't perfect by any means, but she didn't know him well enough to dislike him as much as she evidently did.

He took a thoughtful sip of coffee and glanced at the two boys playing at the computer in the other room. Perched on his favorite stool, Jeffrey was totally involved in his game. His wiry body was taut with concentration, and he held the controls like a fighter pilot at the helm of a jet.

Or a racing car.

Rowe had seen enough news photos of himself in his racing days to see echoes of himself in the child's pose. They looked sufficiently alike to be father and son, he thought, a shiver of something very like longing rippling through him. In fact they looked far too much alike.

He switched his gaze to Kirsten. *Was* it possible they had had an affair six years and nine months ago? He'd been a lot younger and more foolish then. He could barely remember his twenty-second year. A newspaper had cobbled together a series about his father supposedly living in Australia under another identity, and the whole story of his family's loss had been dragged into the headlines anew.

He had refused to talk to the media, but they'd attributed comments to him, anyway. Wanting to fight back, he'd been hampered by the royal family's strict rule never to comment on publicity about themselves. He'd turned his anger inward, partying, drinking and womanizing as if there was no tomorrow. For his father, there hadn't been.

In a fairly short time he had come to his senses, and his life now was far different from those days. He'd been so shocked by his own behavior that he'd given up racing to make a settled life for himself, directing his energy into his business, which now had fingers in many corporate pies. The event-management side that he'd told Kirsten about was only a fraction of what he did.

He liked to think if he'd slept with her during that earlier time, he would remember, but he couldn't be sure. It would certainly explain her anger toward him.

Then again, she could simply be annoyed with him for intruding on her turf. He'd known enough people who thought major sporting events were a reckless waste of resources. But the simple fact was, without a major sporting event such as the Tour de Merrisand,

the trust might not be able to continue its charitable work.

Finishing the coffee, he put the cup down, stood
and stalked to Kirsten's chair. He had to wake her
before he left the house, and the most sensible way
to avoid startling her was to kiss her. Perhaps a kiss
would tell him if he'd tasted her lips before, he
thought, knowing he was rationalizing.

He couldn't help himself, he had to find out.

Mindful of the children in the other room, he restrained himself to the lightest touch of his mouth to
hers, but almost groaned aloud as fire tore through
him. Just as well he had the boys' nearness to stop
him from gathering Kirsten into his arms and crushing
her mouth with his the way he wanted to do.

Her lips parted slightly, roseate and inviting. In her
drowsy state, she began to return the kiss and his
pulse picked up speed in response. Then her eyes flut-
tered open.

Quickly he stepped back, watching her fight
through the cobwebs of her dream. In her sleepy state,
she looked so attractive that temptation became a
whirlpool, threatening to drag him under. The light
taste of her he had allowed himself had only given
him an appetite for more.

She stretched languorously. "I was dreaming."

Should he tell her that she hadn't dreamed his kiss?
She'd probably scratch his eyes out if he did, he decided. At the same time, he wondered if her anger
was real or a defense against his effect on her? Or
was that just wishful thinking?

Coming fully awake, she jerked upright. "I must
have dozed off. I'm sorry, Your Lordship," she said,

running a finger along her lower lip, as if the taste of him lingered there.

The unconscious gesture fired him with desire. "It was Rowe before. And you don't have to apologize for having a busy day."

"Jeffrey and Michael?"

"They're in the other room playing with the computer," he supplied, guessing the reason for her sudden agitation. "Your son is delightful."

His son, too, Kirsten thought, her antipathy toward him returning in a rush. This time it was overlaid by another sensation, a yearning that had nothing to do with Jeffrey. She must still be caught in the traces of her dream, she told herself. Nothing else could explain the surge of pure pleasure she had felt at finding him filling her field of vision as she awoke. In the dream she had imagined Rowe kissing her and, worse, her responding with an ardor she had no business feeling.

It was only a dream, she reminded herself. The shock of his unexpected arrival and now having him in her home must have confused her thinking. When they started working together, she would be better prepared, she assured herself.

He hadn't really kissed her, and she wouldn't have welcomed it if he had. The yearning she'd felt was unrelated to Rowe himself. If she felt anything for him, it was pure dislike for treating Natalie so badly. The reminder enabled her to say coolly, "I really shouldn't take up any more of your time."

He shrugged. "You haven't taken anything I didn't want to give. There's still that foot massage I promised you."

Still in the grip of her dream-induced vulnerability,

she knew if he touched her now, she couldn't answer for the consequences. "I'll be fine. There's no need for you to stay."

For a moment she swore he wanted to, but he said easily, "I recommend a foot bath with some chamomile in the water. And a change of shoes for tomorrow."

The strappy wonders were lying beside her chair where she'd dropped them. If she ever wore them again, it would be to a place where no standing was involved. She didn't want to give him any more excuses to escort her home. "I intend to."

"Then I'll see you at the office tomorrow. Don't get up. I'll see myself out."

She couldn't have gotten up if her life depended on it. Not because of her sore feet, but because she felt like a balloon with all the air let out of it. She must be crazy letting him make himself at home here. What if Jeffrey had innocently said something revealing to him while she was asleep? Had there been time for Rowe to see the resemblance between them?

She didn't know and she couldn't ask. The front door closed behind him, and his presence haunted her for a long time after he'd gone.

Chapter Five

She had told herself she wouldn't let his kiss affect their working relationship, but when Rowe came into her office two days later, the first thing that sprang to her mind was how tantalizing his lips had felt against hers in her dream. She couldn't help wondering how the reality compared.

Much to her annoyance, her intention to be cool and businesslike toward him went flying out the window the moment he loomed over her desk, bringing with him a hint of that wonderful, outdoorsy scent that was obviously the aftershave he favored.

She breathed deeply, telling herself she was bracing for the encounter, and said briskly, "Did we have an appointment this morning?"

His gaze lingered on her as if he, too, was thinking of the fleeting touch of mouth to mouth that was imprinted on her mind like a brand. But he couldn't be. The kiss had been a dream, hadn't it?

"We have an appointment every morning until I get the Tour de Merrisand up and running," he said.

She gestured at the paperwork stacked on her desk. "I don't think I can give you that much time."

He looked as if he would like to sweep the stacks aside. "You don't have a choice. From now on, this project is your top priority, as I know Max has already informed you."

How did he know what had transpired at her meeting with Prince Maxim? Unable to disguise her dislike of holding a sporting event at the castle, she had been surprised when the prince also emphasized the importance of the race to the future of the Merrisand Trust's work with underprivileged children. Of course, Rowe was the prince's cousin, and blood was thicker than water—unless you were Rowe's son, she thought on a welcome surge of anger that helped to dispel the memory of his kiss. In disapproving of the race, she was in a minority here.

Was the race or Rowe himself the reason for her antipathy? She didn't see how she could separate the two. If Rowe had shouldered his responsibilities toward Natalie and their baby, Kirsten might have approached the sporting event with an open mind. As things stood, she couldn't forgive him for turning his back on his child, and it was bound to taint any dealings she had with him.

To avoid meeting his gaze, she shuffled some of the files. "The prince asked me to work with you on the project, but he didn't specify how much time I should set aside from my normal duties."

Rowe braced both hands flat on her desk. "Then let me specify it now. If this race isn't spectacularly successful, all the exhibitions of all the paintings in this castle won't make a damn bit of difference. So I suggest you cancel whatever else you had planned for the rest of the morning.''

She folded her hands primly and made herself look at him. It was an effort not to flinch as she met the determination in his stormy gaze. ''If time is so critical, I'm surprised you waited until now to show up at the office.''

Why had she made such an obvious comment? Now he would guess that she had looked for him all day yesterday, almost convincing herself that she wasn't disappointed when he failed to arrive.

Almost defiantly she had conducted one of the tours herself and been annoyed to find herself keeping one eye on the latecomers, wondering if he would join them as he had before. Wondering or hoping? No amount of assuring herself that she didn't care if he never came back answered the question to her satisfaction.

Rowe regarded her steadily, intrigued by the way the light of challenge danced in her unusual silver-gray eyes. He wasn't about to tell her that he had spent the day holed up in the apartment Max had allocated to him, sketching possible routes for the race, rather than turn up here and deal with Kirsten in person. He wasn't sure why he hadn't wanted to come to the office, but his vivid recollection of kissing her had more to do with it than he wanted it to.

As kisses went, it was hardly earthshaking. More a mere brush of the lips than a real kiss. The trouble was, having tasted her, he wanted more, and that wasn't going to work if they had to spend a lot of time together. He hadn't been exaggerating when he said Merrisand needed this race. Max trusted him to get it right. Having an affair with Kirsten wasn't going to help.

Thinking about her wasn't doing much for his concentration, either, Rowe decided. So he had two choices: call on the self-discipline that had taken him to the top in car racing and work with her as no more than a colleague; or take her to bed as soon as possible and get her out of his system.

His expression must have betrayed his reaction to this thought because Kirsten moved back, looking startled. He hoped to goodness she wasn't telepathic, because his physical response to the idea of taking her to bed had been strong enough to alarm anyone who could read his thoughts. It sure as heck alarmed him.

Contrary to his popular image, he wasn't the playboy he allowed people to think. True enough, he'd had affairs with beautiful women but he hadn't taken anything they weren't willing to give. And he'd said goodbye to them as soon as things got more involved.

A couple had become fixtures for a while, if they possessed intelligence and passion, as well as beauty. But they inevitably turned out to be more interested in his title than in Rowe himself. One of the women he'd genuinely liked had seemed elusive for a time, causing him to pursue her, but it had turned out to be a game. She, too, had been more interested in his title than in him.

Telling himself Kirsten was probably no different didn't help. He couldn't shake the feeling that she knew more about him than she was telling, and what she knew, she didn't particularly like. The mystery only heightened the attraction he could feel pulling at him like a magnet, in spite of his attempts to ignore it.

"I spent yesterday going over plans of the castle and the surrounding estate, mapping out a likely course," he said, not sure why he was explaining himself to her.

She looked nonplussed. "I don't know the first thing about bike races, so I won't be much help with that."

He angled his body onto a corner of her desk, letting one leg swing free. "You can look at my preferred route from the angle of spectators and television cameras to ensure we set up the best vantage points." He felt a rueful grin tug at his mouth. "You can also make sure the cyclists don't run over any historic landmarks."

"Since most of the castle comes under that heading, they can hardly avoid it," she said dryly.

He folded his arms, wondering why he didn't pull royal rank and command her to assist him. For some reason, he wanted her on side, and not only because he found her attractive. He sensed there was a lot more to Kirsten Bond, and he wouldn't rest until he knew what it was. "Then you wouldn't have approved of the carriage races that were run around Merrisand Estate in the late 1700s."

He'd surprised her, he saw when her eyes widened. "I did my homework," he said, enjoying her confusion. "I rather liked reading Great-Great-Great-Great-Grandfather Pierre's account of the wagers he won on those races."

"They were recreation for the royal family," she said, sounding unhappy that he was a step ahead of her.

"And that makes them more noble than the modern equivalent for the masses?"

At his sarcastic tone, a tiny frown etched a V into her forehead. "Horses and carriages are gentler than multigeared racing bikes."

He lifted an eyebrow. "Are you sure about that? According to my forebear's journal, which Max was kind enough to lend to me, the damage to the old castle wall, near the east gate happened during a hard-fought race when Pierre's carriage had an argument with a runaway horse."

She lowered her eyes. "I didn't know."

"Don't tell me you believed the story that the wall was damaged when a princess rolled her carriage on the way to meet the lover her father had forbidden her to see, did you?" She looked away quickly, but not before he had seen the warmth blooming on her cheeks. "You did believe it. I'll bet you even tell visitors the story with appropriately romantic embellishments." He gave a theatrical sigh. "Ah, romance, so much more elegant than the facts."

"You don't have to sneer."

"I'm not, believe me. But you have to admit that if television had existed in my ancestor's day, he'd have built stands to house the spectators and had the races televised, exactly as I intend to do."

He was probably right, she acknowledged to herself reluctantly. She linked her hands on her desktop. "Why are you trying so hard to convince me this event is a good idea? Surely my opinion doesn't matter."

"It does to me. It will be easier to work together if we can get along."

"Can't we agree to differ?" Even as she asked the

question, she knew what his answer would be. Everything about Rowe Sevrin suggested that he was used to getting his way. He'd managed it with Natalie, and Kirsten sensed he wouldn't be happy until he'd won her over, too.

He gave her a lopsided smile that sent shivers down her spine. "I'd much prefer us to agree."

"How can I when I know so little about cycling?"

He uncoiled from her desk and stood up, holding out his hand. "We can remedy that, starting right now."

She hadn't intended to take his hand, wanting as little physical contact with him as possible. But somehow her fingers found their way into his, and the warmth of his touch shot up her arm, the molten stream pooling near her heart. Had his grip not been so firm, she would have jerked her hand free. But he'd pulled her to her feet and was towing her toward the door before she had time to reconsider.

Over her shoulder she shot a desperate look at her crowded desk. "Where are we going? I have work to do here."

"This is work, as well. I'm going to drive you around the Tour de Merrisand circuit and see what you think of the course."

He already knew what she thought—that his plan was an affront to a heritage area. Showing her the course of the event was only going to confirm her worst fears. "You may regret this," she cautioned.

"I doubt it. Unless you don't trust my driving."

It was herself she didn't trust, alone in a car with him. "Having seen you control a car at 280 miles an hour, I don't think I need worry about your driving skills."

He regarded her with renewed interest. "I thought you didn't watch car racing."

She couldn't confess that she had taken an interest in Rowe only because of Natalie. "I caught a glimpse of you on the news once," she said, striving to sound offhand.

He wasn't fooled, she saw by his penetrating gaze. "Enough of a glimpse to note who was driving and how fast I was going?"

"My sister used to be a fan. She tried to explain it all to me."

Something in her tone caught his attention. "Used to be?"

A lump clogged Kirsten's throat. "She died six and a half years ago."

"I'm sorry for your loss."

He sounded sincere. Would he feel the same way if he knew that her sister had been his one-time lover and mother of his child?

"She must have been young. Was it illness or accident?"

She ducked her head, blinking hard to banish the threat of tears. "An accident at a sporting event. I'd rather not talk about it." Especially not to him.

He stopped beside the old castle wall, his hand under her chin bringing her head up. "That explains your reluctance to be involved with such events," he said. "I was starting to think *I* was the problem."

To distract herself from the unsettling effect of his touch, she focused on the mossy stones, finding along the brickwork the marks of the two-hundred-year-old accident she had once thought so romantic. Not anymore. People didn't change, she thought. Not Rowe's great-great-great-great grandfather, and not Rowe himself. "I hardly know you," she said on a heavy sigh. "Prince Maxim asked me to work with you, and I will to the best of my ability."

He let her go. "But he couldn't order you to get along with me."

"I didn't know it was a job requirement."

"It isn't, but we'll be putting in some long hours on this project. They'll be easier if we aren't constantly at each other's throats."

The thought of working into the night alongside him set her nerves on edge. For an instant she thought seriously about resigning from her job rather than put herself through that. But Rowe had already taken enough from her. She wasn't going to let him take anything more.

"Very well, we'll declare a truce," she said as calmly as she could.

He regarded her suspiciously. "Giving in so easily?"

"Yielding to the logic of the situation. I may never be a sports fan, but so we can work together effectively, I'll try to understand what you do and why you do it." If only he could do the same for her, but without explaining about her sister and revealing his relationship to Jeffrey, that wasn't going to happen.

"I've already told you why I'm here," he reminded her.

She shook her head. "I don't mean the fund-raising effort. I meant, why you would risk your life manhandling a piece of machinery around a track to show the world how fast you can go."

He considered her question. "I could give the same answer the mountaineers give—because it's there—but it's more personal. My birthright meant that I had no need to earn a living. I wanted to pit myself against something that wasn't handed to me on a plate. When I was nineteen, I was given the chance to drive a Formula One car. After the training I was given and the race itself, I knew I'd found my challenge. Speed is a great leveler. When you're on the racetrack, being royal doesn't win races or keep you alive. You're on your own.''

His answer surprised her. She had thought his status gave him an automatic edge in whatever he did. She should have seen that it could open the way for him, but the outcome had depended entirely on Rowe himself. It wasn't how she wanted to see him, but there was no avoiding it. She couldn't help asking, ''What did your family think about your choice of career?''

He walked on toward the east gate, taking her arm so naturally that they had traveled a few steps before she noticed. Telling herself she should pull her arm free, she couldn't bring herself to do it. What kind of sister to Natalie that made her, she wasn't sure, but she found herself enjoying the sensation of being arm in arm with him.

''My mother was horrified,'' he said after a thoughtful pause. ''After losing my father, she wanted me to do something secure and predictable. But my father's disappearance made me aware of how brief life can be. I didn't want it passing me by while I stayed safe behind a desk.''

Was that why he had made love with Natalie? Kirsten could even understand his need to make the most of a life made all the more precious by his father's disappearance. But she couldn't understand how he could ignore the birth of his own child.

Hardening her heart, she unhooked her arm from his and took a step to put some distance between them. It was too little, too late. He stopped beside a car parked in a visitor's space alongside the royal barracks.

"Yours?" she asked. When he nodded, her heart sank. She should have expected a former racing-car driver to favor a sports car, but the two-seater vehicle looked alarmingly compact. Rowe was a big man. She wasn't ready to deal with sharing such a small space with him.

He misread her expression as fear. "Don't worry, we won't be hitting three hundred miles an hour today. I only did it a couple of times myself, and that was under race conditions on a perfect driving surface. Normally I drive far more sedately, I promise."

He unlocked the doors with a remote control and opened the passenger side for her. She slid into the seat, finding it every bit as confined as she'd feared. She was practically sitting on the road, and when Rowe folded his considerable length into the driver's seat, they were shoulder to shoulder.

"Isn't this car a bit small for you?" she asked uneasily.

He grinned, barely glancing at the controls as he gunned the ignition with a skill born of long experience. The car settled into a low growl and moved off so smoothly she hardly felt the motion. "You've obviously never levered yourself into the driving compartment of a Formula One car. This is spacious by comparison."

It didn't feel spacious to her. She hugged her door as closely as possible, but the heat from his body radiated through her. Every time he changed gears, his arm brushed her thigh, the sensation alarmingly intimate. To distract herself she asked, ''Is this the kind of car you used to race?''

He shook his head. ''This is a prototype I designed for my own enjoyment.''

''You designed this?'' No wonder the driver's seat fitted him like a glove.

''Don't sound so surprised. I have other talents besides being able to officiate at royal functions and drive ridiculously fast.''

Thinking what his other talents might be, she felt heat rush into her face and turned her head away. Groups of visitors to the castle were regarding them with interest, she saw. Was it the car, or because Rowe was at the wheel? He was the attraction, she decided. The car was unique, but it wasn't ostentatious, obviously designed more for his own driving needs than to show off. But Rowe himself would command attention no matter what kind of car he drove.

Not used to being the center of attention away from her work, Kirsten breathed more easily when Rowe drove through the east gate past the guard post and turned into the vast, forested area known as the great park. The guards recognized the viscount and saluted, then one of them operated a striped barrier to let them into the park.

Apart from twice-yearly open days and charitable functions, the park was closed to the public. The peace that descended was almost palpable as Rowe steered along the road winding between groves of ancient trees. The bustle of the castle receded. Soon there were no other people within sight. They could have been miles from civilization.

She released a breath she hadn't been aware of holding. As an employee of the castle, she was permitted to use the park, and she liked to bring Jeffrey here for picnics and ball games. "I love this place."

Rowe nodded, slowing the car as if the surroundings were affecting him, too. "It is peaceful, although I have trouble looking at this road without seeing Great-Great-Great-Great-Grandfather Pierre's horse-drawn carriages galloping along it."

"The forest would have been denser then, probably full of wildlife. Now I know where some of the trophies in the tower hall must have come from, poor things."

Rowe laughed, the warm sound sending a shiver along her spine. "Eighteenth-century roadkill. There's a thought."

"What wildlife there is in the forest stays well away from the road these days," she went on, aware that she was chattering to keep from focusing on his closeness. "With the encroachment of residential areas on the park fringes, the sun deer prefer the seclusion of the home park. I'm glad. They're such beautiful, gentle creatures."

"When I lived at the castle as a child, I used to feed the deer by hand," he said. "My grandfather told me they had to be looked after as the faunal emblem of Carramer, but to me they were my friends. I told everyone I was going to work in the deer sanctuary when I grew up."

She could imagine him wanting to help preserve the rare sun deer. He must have been as pleased as she was to learn that they hadn't been hunted for a century. "Then you drove in the Formula One."

He slanted a smile at her. "You have to admit, there isn't much comparison."

"Maybe to a teenage boy."

His sigh gusted between them. "But not to a woman who thinks the Tour de Merrisand amounts to cultural vandalism."

"I didn't say that."

"But you're thinking it."

She knew her expression gave her away. "I think something like a medieval fair would be more fitting in this setting."

"Even though your fair would make peanuts for the Merrisand Trust?"

"Why does everything come down to money?"

"Because like it or not, the world runs on money. If it didn't, there would be no need for a body like the trust."

"You've made your point," she conceded. "I'll do what I can to make this plan work…for the sake of the trust." It didn't mean she had to like Rowe or get involved with him beyond a business relationship, but opposing him wasn't going to change his mind. She had a feeling nothing could do that.

He brought the car to a smooth stop in a shaded clearing and turned, one long-fingered hand resting on the wheel as he slewed his body around to look at her. "Well, well. Wonders will never cease. I was starting to think you were going to fight me every step of the way."

He sounded almost disappointed, she thought in confusion. "Prince Maxim made his wishes clear. I'm hardly in a position to oppose either of you."

His fingers played lightly along her forearm. "And that's the only reason you've decided to help me?"

Kirsten felt her heartbeat quicken. She wanted to move away, but there was nowhere to go. He seemed hardly aware of touching her. Perhaps it was something he did without thinking. She wished she could stop herself from thinking, from feeling, but a maelstrom of emotion whirled inside her, created by his featherlight caress. "What other reason could I have?" she asked unsteadily.

She saw his eyebrow lift and he said, "I've been waiting for you to tell me."

The air thinned suddenly, and she had to struggle to breathe. "There's nothing to tell."

He drew a finger lightly down the side of her face, making her tremble. "No? Then why have you been looking at me as if I were the devil incarnate since the moment I joined your tour?"

Chapter Six

A moment earlier, she had welcomed the silence of the forest. Now she wished for noise and people around her to dispel the rapidly thickening atmosphere between them. "You're imagining things," she insisted.

He caught her hand and held it against his chest so she felt the steady thrum of his heart through his finely woven shirt. Was he going to kiss her hand again? Instead, he rested two fingers on her wrist. "Am I imagining the way your pulse is throbbing like a trapped bird?"

She couldn't deny what he could feel for himself, so she turned her head away, although her awareness remained on the heat of his hands around hers. Her throat felt raw, and speaking was a challenge. "Shouldn't we get back to the office?"

"In a couple of months the cyclists will follow this road, so in a way we're in the office. Right now, I'm more interested in what you know about me—or think you know.''

She strove to normalize her tone. "I know your biographical details, as I do all the royal family connected with Merrisand Castle. It's my job to know.''

''And on the basis of a few facts, you've taken a violent dislike to me? I would have expected better from you, Kirsten.''

She shot him an angry look. "You don't know me, either, certainly not enough to judge me.''

He grazed his chin against her knuckles, the faintly rasping sensation sending pinpricks of desire through her. "I know you're a beautiful, sensual woman who is passionate about her job and her child. Have you any idea how attractive I find that?''

It was difficult to think when her mind was so at odds with her physical responses. She took refuge in annoyance. "Next thing, you'll be telling me how beautiful I look when I'm angry.'' How many women besides Natalie had fallen for such hackneyed lines?

"I can't, because you're not angry. You seem to want me to think you are, but I sense that you feel as much for me as I do for you. You're fighting it for some reason. I want to know the reason.''

She tossed her head, real anger coursing through her now, but at herself for letting him see how she felt. She should have been cold and distant, then he would have had no weapon to use against her. "You have a high opinion of yourself,'' she snapped.

Her anger slid off him. "When everyone calls you 'Your Lordship' and waits on you hand and foot from the moment you're born, it's difficult not to have a high opinion of yourself.''

"I didn't mean because you're royal. I meant because…'' Aware of how close she was to flinging the truth in his face, she clamped her mouth shut.

"Yes?" he said in a low, dangerous tone. "You were going to say…"

"It's a beautiful day and this setting is far too lovely to waste on a pointless argument," she said defiantly. Let him make what he would of that.

"You're right," he surprised her by saying. "It's far too lovely to waste."

Before she could react, he slid an arm around her shoulders and pulled her against him, trapping her free hand against his chest. His heartbeat was far from steady now, she noticed in the strange sense of time-lessness that accompanied the moment.

Caught in the circle of his arms, she felt no fear. Even her anger felt muted. There was only a tremulous sense of excitement accompanying the certainty that he was going to kiss her.

The forest retreated into a green blur, the birdsong muting, so she was aware only of the cramped interior of the car and Rowe's hold on her. As her thoughts spun, she found her lips parting in instant, unthinking response.

Trying to tell herself that Rowe was a danger to everything she held dear didn't help. When he took her mouth, desire surged through her like an incoming tide, flooding her with needs she'd barely acknowledged since taking over, first Natalie's care, and now Jeffrey's.

Rowe's hold on her firmed as he deepened the kiss, and she slid her free arm up around his neck, feeling muscle cord under her fingers. The waves swirled around her, threatening to close over her head. She was drowning in a sea of his creation. He murmured her name, and the sound was like a caress. She felt a low moan start in her throat and heard herself whisper his name.

She had known this moment would come from her first sight of him at the back of the tour group. No amount of reasoning with herself was going to prevent it or change its course. Some things were meant to be. She just hadn't expected it to happen so swiftly or irresistibly, thinking her innate common sense would enable her to resist temptation when it came.

The blood roared in her ears, echoing the sound of the wind in the trees around them. Rowe's mouth was shaping hers as the trees were shaped by the wind. His hand slid over her shirt, resting on the warm fullness of her breasts. She nestled against him, letting him find and surround her with his warmth. Where was her resistance now?

Gone with the wind, she thought on a fresh surge of desire. Lost among the trees, as elusive as the sun deer. She would never recapture her ability to resist Rowe. He would take her wherever he wanted them to go, and she would allow it because she needed what he was offering her so much that she was willing to risk everything for it.

How much she risked gradually seeped into her awareness like a cold rain carried on the wind of desire. She shivered, reality chilling her as rapidly as desire had heated her. For Jeffrey's sake, if not for her own, she had to find the strength to resist Rowe. She forced out a strangled no.

He released her and she moved away as far as the limited space would allow, which was not nearly far enough. Tidying her clothes, her hands felt unsteady, and she breathed hard as if deprived of oxygen for a long while.

He glared at her. "You can't deny you wanted me to touch you?"

She brushed strands of hair out of her eyes, denying herself the right to hide behind them. He might be royal and she a commoner, but they were equal in *this*. He had a right to know where he stood. She only wished he didn't look so warrior-fierce, like one of the portraits of his ancestors in the castle galleries. His look made desire claw at her, tempting her anew. "I did want it, but I shouldn't have."

He scrubbed a hand over his chin. "Why the hell not? Neither of us is married." His glare intensified. "You're not committed to anyone, are you? Is it Jeffrey's father?"

The truth of this must have been reflected in her gaze because Rowe's expression softened. "I should have thought of that before. Did he hurt you badly, Kirsten?"

"It's really none of your business."

"The last few minutes makes it my business. If you had refused to kiss me, I might have accepted that you don't want to get involved. But your response betrayed you. You recognized what's between us as soon as we met, as did I. It was only a matter of time before we acted on it, and you knew that, too, didn't you."

She nodded, not trusting herself to convince him with a lie. Choosing her words with care, she said, "Jeffrey's father never loved me."

"And you didn't find out until you were pregnant?" His long fingers tightened their grip on the leather steering wheel. "I would never do such a thing to you, Kirsten."

The savage intensity in his assertion made it difficult to remember that it was exactly what he had done to her sister. He had led Natalie to think he cared about her, made love to her, then abandoned her when she told him she was expecting his child. "It doesn't matter," Kirsten said tonelessly. "After Jeffrey was born I promised myself not to get involved with anyone while he depends on me."

He began to drum silently on the wheel. "That's very noble of you. Understandable, even." He directed a blazing look at her. "But what if love comes your way in that time? Will you let it slip away, perhaps never to be recaptured, to keep a bargain that might not be in your son's best interests?"

White-hot anger surged through her. "You don't have any idea what's best for my son."

"I'm not sure you do, either. Cocooning him in your own little world won't give you back what his father took from you."

His arrogance took her breath away. He was the last person entitled to judge her. "I don't use Jeffrey as a substitute for anything. Our life is fine as it is." *Was until you came along,* she thought in mounting despair.

"I'm not going to let this end here," he vowed. "What's between us can't be denied."

"There's nothing between us." She wouldn't let there be.

"We'll discuss it again tomorrow when I take Jeffrey kite flying. I made him a promise and I always keep my word."

To her, as well as to her son, she read into this. "You don't have to. I'll take him myself."

She saw him pull in a deep breath. "I won't be shut out so easily. I realize Jeffrey's father must have hurt you badly, but I'm not him and I won't be treated as if I were."

"Why can't we work together and leave things at that?" she appealed.

"I've asked myself the same question and I still don't have an answer. All I know is after years of allowing myself only physical relationships, for the first time I want something more. Everything started changing the day I met you and your son. But if you can tell me honestly that you don't want my attention, I'll accept the verdict. We'll work together as if the last few minutes never happened, and we'll never find out what we could have been to one another."

He couldn't be anything to her; she wouldn't let him. She didn't want her mother's life, loving a man who professed to love her, then strayed as soon as the first bloom of passion was spent. Everything she knew about Rowe suggested he was like that. The risk was too great.

She turned her head stiffly, her cheek brushing the hand tangled in her hair. The touch was all it took to stifle the denial she tried to utter. He let the silence go on for a long time before giving a slight smile. "I thought so. For what it's worth, I think you've made the right decision. I can't promise to go slowly. The attraction between us is too strong for that. But I can promise that things will be different from how they were with Jeffrey's father."

"How can you be sure?" she asked wildly. He didn't know it, but as her son's father, he *couldn't* be different. She wondered how stupid she had been not to deny him when she had the chance. Why hadn't she?

He let his hand trail through her hair before taking the wheel again. "I'm sure because I know myself. Don't be fooled by what you think you know about me, Kirsten. Listen to your heart."

She had done that, and look where it had gotten her. By her silence, she had agreed to explore a relationship with him when it was the last thing she should have done. The closer he came to her, the more chance there was that he would learn her son's secret, then what would happen? He may have ignored the baby's birth, but that didn't mean he wouldn't want to claim Jeffrey as his heir now, especially with Natalie gone. What on earth had Kirsten unleashed?

It was too late to recant. Rowe had restarted the car and now he drove back onto the road, making observations about the Tour de Merrisand as if the kiss had never happened. She heard him say something about siting a grandstand in the clearing, but was too preoccupied with her own worries to pay full attention. She hoped fervently that something would come up to prevent him from taking Jeffrey kite flying tomorrow.

She should have known life wasn't that simple or kind. Her tension mounted as she tidied the kitchen. Jeffrey was kneeling on the window seat that gave him a view of the village green. Suddenly he jumped up and ran for the door. "He's here. Viscount Aragon is here."

"Jeffrey, wait." But the child had already

wrenched open the front door, giving her no time to gather her wits.

Rowe's gaze roved appreciatively over her navy pants and navy-and-white-striped T-shirt. A matching headband tamed her mass of red curls. She had told herself she wasn't dressing to please him. Now she wondered.

"I'll get my kite, Mister Viscount," Jeffrey told him excitedly.

Rowe hunkered down to the little boy's level, the sight of the two dark heads close together making her breath catch. "Why don't you call me Rowe, since we're going to be friends?"

Jeffrey screwed up his face. "Isn't your name Viscount?"

"That's my title, like prince or princess."

Jeffrey looked at Kirsten. "Do I have a title, too?"

"Of course," Rowe said.

Her heart almost stopped. Under different circumstances, Jeffrey would have been the next viscount.

Before she could drag an answer out of her whirling thoughts, Rowe said, "Your title is Master Bond."

Jeffrey giggled. "That's funny. Mommy says I can be Jeff or Jeffrey."

Rowe looked at her, the galvanic moment of eye contact reminding her of the power of his kiss. Not that she had forgotten an instant of it. She wondered if she looked like a woman with barely four hours' sleep behind her. He looked amazing. She doubted if he had stayed awake thinking of her, as she had done with him.

She'd tried to convince herself that he wasn't special. In the hours before dawn, it had seemed possible.

Faced with the reality, she faltered. Logic told her he was the enemy, but everything about him sent messages of desire to the primitive part of her brain that knew only how to want. The tight fit of his dark jeans as he crouched beside the child. The way his hair was mussed by the breeze, the collar of his cream open-necked shirt turning up a little, making her itch to smooth it down, all spoke to parts of her she had suppressed in order to be the mother Jeffrey needed.

Rowe returned his attention to her son. "Which name do you like best?"

The child shrugged.

"I have two names, as well," Rowe said. "Romain is my full name, but I like to be called Rowe."

"Why?" Jeffery asked.

Kirsten ruffled her son's hair. "Don't ask so many questions. Go get your kite."

"It's in my room." He grabbed Rowe's hand. "Do you want to see my room?"

"I'm sure Rowe doesn't…" She was talking to herself. Jeffrey had already dragged Rowe to the stairs. Over his shoulder he gave her a rueful glance and let the child lead him up them.

Knowing she should follow, she hesitated. How had Rowe managed to get so close to her and her son in such a short time? She'd only known him for a couple of days, but it seemed like much longer.

Having her sister's description of him to draw on didn't account for Kirsten's feeling that she had known Rowe forever. The feeling was primitive and personal, its power undeniable.

Suddenly she remembered the photo of herself and Natalie in Jeffrey's room. Heart pounding, she raced up the stairs.

Rowe was on the floor, helping Jeffrey to place model cars on a figure-eight track she had given him last Christmas. An unintended link between father and son, she thought, as she pushed Jeffrey's old teddy bear in front of the photo, her hands shaking with the nearness of the miss. This would have to stop. She couldn't be around Rowe without worrying that he would discover his link with Jeffrey.

She couldn't be around Rowe, period. The damage to her peace of mind was too much. That the damage was to the sexual part of herself that she had carefully walled off, she hated to think, but it was closer to the truth. He made her feel things, want things, she had no business feeling and wanting, especially with him.

"Enough of the course setup. Let's get racing," Rowe said.

Jeffrey pressed buttons on his hand control and one of the cars leaped away from the starting grid. Rowe took his time starting the other car, she noticed. By then Jeffrey's car was halfway around the track. His consideration for the child's feelings ate at her resistance. He cheered as Jeffrey's car raced over the finish line. "That's a 350-point win at least."

Jeffrey picked up his car and studied it. "How do you know that?"

"Every track you race on in a season gets you points toward winning that year's championship," Rowe explained. "Most street circuits are worth up to 270 points, but some tracks have special-event status and earn higher points. I'm sure this track has special status."

"I'm going to be a racing-car driver when I grow up," Jeffrey said confidently.

Her heart sank. Were his genes the only thing to

have a say in his future? "There's plenty of time to think about that," Rowe told him as he helped the child to his feet. "Right now, we have a kite to fly."

Before they took Jeffrey's kite out to the village green, she would have bet money that nothing could get the flimsy craft airborne. She had reckoned without Rowe's determination.

He had brought with him a roll of special string and a T-shaped hand control, and he tied the paper kite to the string before showing Jeffrey how to launch it into the air. To her amazement, the confection of paper, wood and glue caught the breeze and hovered high overhead, making a paper rainbow, the imperfections invisible.

"Look, Mommy, it's flying a lot higher than it did in school," Jeffrey cried as he ran with his toy, making it swoop and dive in the air.

"Wonders will never cease," she murmured. Impulsively she touched Rowe's arm. "Thank you."

His hand covered hers. "My pleasure."

"You sound as if you mean that."

He raised an eyebrow at her. "This isn't only for Jeffrey, Kirsten. I'm having the time of my life helping him. He's a terrific child. You can be proud of him."

"I've simply nurtured what nature gave him," she insisted, feeling herself flush. Talking to Rowe about Jeffrey was risky, but she couldn't seem to avoid it. Perhaps that explained her feeling of connection to the viscount, she thought.

At the same time she knew it wasn't the whole explanation. Desire for him rushed through her, hot and potent. If he hadn't been touching her hand, she would have moved away. Not that distance would change anything. He hadn't been in her room last night, but he might as well have been, given the way he dominated her thoughts.

"You're frowning. What's wrong now?" he asked.

Since she could hardly admit the truth, she said, "I'm wondering how I'm going to tear Jeffrey away from kite flying. We're going to the zoo early tomorrow and I have food to prepare for a picnic." She seized on the excuse to get away.

"You go ahead. I'll keep an eye on him and bring him back before sunset."

Leaving Jeffrey alone with Rowe hadn't been part of her plan. "It's kind of you, but I can't take up any more of your time."

"I'm happy to help. You'll get more done at home on your own."

He pushed a lock of dark hair off his forehead, reminding her so much of Jeffrey that her heart skipped a beat. She shook her head, fear for her son making her tone harsh. "Thank you, but no."

She read disappointment in his gaze. "You're the boss, in this at least." He hesitated uncharacteristically. "I was going to ask you both out to dinner later."

Her feeling of imminent danger returned in full measure. For herself or Jeffrey? She wished she could sort it out. "I've already planned dinner." No way was she issuing an invitation for him to join them, although she found herself wanting to.

"You can't stave off what's between us forever," he said, startling her.

"I'm not staving off anything," she lied. "You can't burst into my life and expect me to rearrange everything."

"I don't expect you to rearrange anything on my account, Kirsten, only to make a little room for what could be."

"You're assuming I want to."

His intense gaze locked with hers, refusing to let her look away. "Your kiss told me you want to. The question between us isn't *if* you'll let me in, but when."

That royal certainty again. If only she possessed a fraction of it, enough to tell him he was wrong. She tried to summon the denial without success, and his confident smile told her he knew it.

The paper kite had slumped to earth, a lot like Kirsten's spirits. Rowe went to help get the toy airborne again, leaving her alone with the premonition that he would find a way into her life. She was afraid they had already taken the first, irrevocable steps.

Chapter Seven

Keeping busy had always been Kirsten's antidote to worry. Rowe's arrival had also increased her workload to the point where the following week brought her little time to think about how to deal with him on a personal level, and for that she was grateful.

His vow to become part of her life nagged at her, for her son's sake and her own. Knowing what kind of man Rowe was, she'd be crazy to allow it, but when had human emotions ever made much sense?

Several exhibitions were coming up at the castle galleries. The one opening in a few weeks featured the first European explorers to visit Carramer. She was focusing on the modern phase of the kingdom's history, beginning in the early 1600s when the Dutch explorers Schouten and Lemaire visited the islands. They were followed by Tasman, Cook, La Perouse and Bligh. The Carramer they visited was already thriving, the present monarchy tracing its origins back a thousand years.

Fortunately, the encounters with the Europeans had been friendly, leading to a wave of aristocratic French settlers known as the Idealists, who had seen Carramer as a haven from the approaching revolution. Their influence had shaped the Carramer Kirsten knew today. She wanted to put together a display that would capture these turning points in her country's history.

In the royal family's collection, there was no shortage of wonderful material including priceless maps, charts, journals and artifacts from the voyagers reaching the kingdom's shores. Her biggest challenge was deciding what to include and what to leave out.

Later in the year, as a counterpoint to the explorers, Kirsten was planning an exhibition on the Mayat culture that had existed in the islands in prehistory. She was already researching the royal family's Mayat treasures and shaping the result in her mind.

Then there was the wretched cycling race that Rowe was bringing together with her assistance. Professionally, she had to admire his efficiency. In only a few days he had persuaded several famous athletes to participate. He was already roughing out a plan to convince the world's media to spend vast sums of money for the broadcast rights.

Her specialty was cajoling sponsors to become involved, and she was proud of having obtained an expression of interest from an international corporation with her first call. She was determined to do her job regardless of her feelings about the race.

Or Rowe, for that matter.

She frowned when he intruded on her thoughts, as he had done far too frequently this week. He was again driving around the route he wanted the race to follow, fine-tuning his plans. She had to admit, he was thorough. A week ago she hadn't believed it would be possible to stage a major cycling race through the castle grounds without disturbing the historic precinct. Now she conceded the ingenuity of his plan.

He intended the race to start under the east gate, then pass between the Audience Chamber and the old castle wall. The course would then skirt the orchid terraces and the state apartments, emerge at the west gate, and travel through the great park. The cyclists would do laps of the six-mile course until the flag was lowered at the finishing line below Parade Hill.

The two royals most closely associated with the castle, Prince Maxim and his sister, Princess Giselle, would attend the race, and Eduard, Marquis of Merrisand would present the trophies, making the occasion a glittering one for the media.

It was up to Kirsten to decide where to locate the royal box and the media facilities, and where the public vantage points should be set up. Although part of her still revolted against the idea of holding a commercial sporting event within the castle precinct, Rowe's enthusiasm was catching. During the past few days, she had found herself actually enjoying the involvement. If she hadn't been worried that Rowe might somehow stumble on Jeffrey's secret, she would have almost looked forward to the race.

She didn't like to think she was worried on her own account, because of the easy way Rowe had insinuated himself into her working life. Or the way her thoughts were haunted by him when she was alone at night.

She knew what kind of man he was. His injunction not to believe what she thought she knew about him, but follow her heart, was exactly what her father would have said. Kirsten had always thought she would be immune to such blandishments, but where Rowe was concerned, it seemed she was no more discerning than her mother.

So she wasn't surprised to feel her heart take a sudden leap when he walked into her office. His hair was windblown from driving with the top down, she assumed, and his face looked flushed with sun or exhilaration or both.

"You should have come with me—it's a fantastic morning," he said, hitching one hip onto the corner of her desk.

She rescued a pile of files before they could slide to the floor. "I had a lot to do here."

He frowned. "Don't tell me you missed lunch again."

"Okay I won't tell you."

"You won't be much use to me if you let yourself waste away."

She gave him a whithering look. "I've managed to be quite useful, even in my dangerously weakened state."

He folded his arms across his broad chest, his disturbingly male aura threatening her composure. "Can't argue with that. I'm pleased to see you throwing yourself into the project."

"Considering my lack of enthusiasm for it," she added, reading his mind.

He smiled, which sent her pulse racing. "I'd love to see what you can do when your heart's in it."

Keep your mind on the work, she ordered herself. "It's in the Voyager exhibition and the Mayat retrospective."

He picked up the Mayat file and began to leaf through it, pausing at photographs of the ancient artifacts she planned to show. Looking up, he said, "So I heard from Max and Giselle. They think the sun shines out of your eyes."

And what about you, Rowe? She told herself it was enough that the prince and princess appreciated her efforts. What Rowe thought didn't matter. She wished he wouldn't *loom* over her so much, scrambling her thoughts. There were plenty of visitors' chairs in her office. Why didn't he use one of them, instead of taking over her desk?

Watching him read the file, she was afraid her desk wasn't the only thing he had taken over. Rarely an hour went by when she didn't think about him. Was it only because they were working fairly closely together?

Wanting to banish the feeling, she stood up. "I have to go."

He replaced the file on the desk. "Haven't you left it late to collect Jeffrey from school?"

"It's my neighbor Shara's day to do it. He'll play with his friend Michael until dinnertime."

He looked pleased. "So there's no rush, is there?"

Why had she told him about the arrangement with Shara? Now she had no excuse to get away. If she hadn't, he might have offered to accompany her. Twice this week he had walked with her as far as the Castle School, and she hadn't missed the speculative looks the other parents directed her way. Rowe didn't seem to care, but that fitted what she knew about him. He was used to being the subject of gossip, but she preferred not to be seen as one of his conquests.

Jeffrey had no such qualms. He was plainly delighted to see the viscount, taking his hand and chatting to him about his day as if it was the most natural thing in the world. It was, she thought with a pang, only her son didn't know it. Not for the first time, she wondered if she was doing the right thing by keeping them apart.

For Jeffrey's sake, she had no choice. Raising a child was a lifetime commitment, not something Rowe could take on and abandon when the novelty wore off. Jeffrey would be devastated. Better for him never to know the truth than become attached to Rowe and get hurt when he moved on.

"I still have to go," she insisted. "I don't want to impose on Shara for too long. Her husband is doing enough taking Jeffrey and Michael fishing this weekend."

As soon as she saw Rowe's eyes gleam, she could have bitten her tongue off. Now he knew she was free for the next two days. Slip of the tongue? Or a message her wayward mind wanted to send him. She wished she knew.

She held her breath as his gaze deepened. "I won't keep you, then. The weather forecast is perfect for a fishing trip."

Surely she wasn't disappointed that he hadn't homed in on her admission, was she? Unless he didn't want to. Perhaps he was only pursuing her for his own amusement, toying with her the way a cat did one of the tiny lizards that roamed the castle grounds. As long as she was unavailable, he could charm her all he liked. Bitterness left a sour taste in her mouth. Stupid, she told herself. What else did she expect from him?

By the time she was ready to go, he had returned

to his own office and was immersed in his computer. He looked distracted, nodding as she wished him a good weekend.

"You have a good one yourself, Kirsten," she murmured sarcastically to herself as she walked out. It was foolish to feel depressed at the prospect of a free weekend ahead. Tomorrow she would go shopping, have her hair done, then order pizza and watch a romantic movie. Jeffrey tended to make funny noises during what he called the smooching bits, spoiling the mood somewhat.

Feeling better, she headed home to face the chaos of fishing gear and backpacks, pack enough picnic food for ten children, knowing it would all be gone by Sunday, and try to get her overexcited child to sleep at a reasonable hour.

After seeing the campers off the next morning, she felt too tired to go shopping, but decided to indulge herself at the hairdresser. Two hours later she emerged, wondering if she'd done the right thing.

Her hairdresser, Kathleen, had cut two inches off the length, and added highlights so that Kirsten's hair glinted a vibrant copper in the morning sunshine. She felt lighter, the hair swaying around her face in a silken curtain. She hadn't realized how long she had let it grow until the hairdresser trimmed it back to shoulder-length.

Since they were both free for the weekend, she had arranged to meet Shara for lunch at an outdoor café in the town that sprawled outside the castle walls. Seeing Kirsten, her neighbor smiled her approval. "You look fantastic. I love the color."

Kirsten joined her at the table, aware that the new

style complemented her apple-green top and white linen pants. "You don't think the color's too strong?"

The beautiful, dark-skinned woman leaned closer. "Honey, with a man like Rowe Sevrin in your life, strong is just what you need."

"Rowe Sevrin isn't in my life. I only work with him."

Shara grinned. "Who helps pick up your son from school, then stays around. I had a colleague like that once, and I ended up marrying him."

Kirsten felt herself color. "This isn't the same. Rowe is staying at the state apartments, so the school is on his way home. After the race, he'll return to Solano."

Shara studied the menu, saying without looking up, "I believe they have a new specialty here. It's called flying pig."

"Shara!"

The black woman rested her chin on one hand. "We've known each other how long?"

Shara, who could trace her family almost back to the original inhabitants of Carramer, was already employed at the castle as Princess Giselle's personal assistant when Kirsten came to work there. Sharing an interest in history, she and Shara had soon become friends. "Quite a few years."

"Then give me credit for knowing when you're attracted to a man. You may not want to admit it, but all the signs are there."

"I can't be. I have Jeffrey to consider."

Shara paused to place her order with the waiter, looking pleased when Kirsten said she would also have the seafood basket and an iced coffee. "That's what we need—calories." Then she turned back to her friend. "You do consider Jeffrey. You've done a great job with him. But part of taking care of him is making sure you have a life, too."

Kirsten gestured around her. "I have a life. I don't need a man to make it complete." Especially not a man like Rowe.

"Who said anything about complete? How about more fun? More passionate?" Her friend's eyes gleamed. "For the first two years of our marriage, Michael was away at university in Solano studying for an advanced degree in horticulture. I felt so deprived I started to think I was sickening for something. I was—him."

How could you miss something you'd never had? Shara also believed that Kirsten was Jeffrey's mother and thought Kirsten knew exactly what she was talking about. What would she say if Kirsten confessed that she was a virgin? The world's oldest, she suspected sometimes.

Waiting for someone special might be considered eccentric these days, but she was comfortable with her choice, except during discussions like this one. She envied Shara her relationship with Michael. Despite their different backgrounds, they were obviously still in love after years of marriage and a child. What would that be like?

Her sigh wasn't lost on Shara. Before the other woman could pick up on it, Kirsten changed the subject, determindly talking about other things until their lunch arrived.

Flicking open her napkin, Shara said, "Calories first, then we talk about how to deal with your other deprivation."

Kirsten laughed uneasily. "I am not deprived." How did one tell?

Over a forkful of succulent lobster, Shara grinned. "How can you not be? You're a beautiful, sexy woman. The viscount sure seems smitten."

Hearing herself called sexy, Kirsten almost choked on a mouthful of ocean trout. She saw herself as bookish and practical, a single mother in every way that mattered. Natalie had been the beautiful, sexy one in the family. "Maybe I *will* order that flying pig," she said.

Shara laughed, but took the hint and changed the subject. Slowly Kirsten started to relax. She might change her mind and go shopping today, after all.

Twice that afternoon, as he put in a few extra hours at the office, Rowe found himself thinking of reasons he needed to consult Kirsten. Twice he managed to convince himself the questions could wait until Monday.

The third time, he faced facts. He wanted to see her. But would she want to see him? She hadn't wanted him to know that she was spending the weekend alone. Although she'd masked it quickly, he hadn't missed her appalled expression after she inadvertently revealed that Jeffrey would be away on a fishing trip. She was just as likely to slam the door in Rowe's face as invite him in.

He snapped the computer off. Only one way to find out.

He hadn't reckoned on her being out when he arrived at her house. On a date? The idea made him frown as he paced her neat front porch. Although they were still within the castle grounds, from here the sounds of visitors and the palace guard were muted. A screen of greenery lay between the retainers' cottages and the rest of the castle, hiding it from view.

If he looked up he could see the castle walls topped by the Merrisand flag, but at this level he could have been in a country village miles from anywhere. It felt peaceful. The cottages were identical, but he admired the way Kirsten had added pots of vibrantly colored orchids and a white-painted park bench to give her house a cozy individuality.

She hadn't talked about a man in her life, but that didn't signify. Jeffrey had to have come from somewhere. Rage flashed through him, astonishing him with its intensity. What kind of man could father a child like Jeffrey, then abandon him? Kirsten could have been the one who walked out, but Rowe doubted it. She wasn't the type to give up easily.

When had he become an expert on Kirsten and her son? He wasn't, he acknowledged, but he wanted to be. He didn't only want to take her to bed, although heaven knew, that desire sent his hormones into overdrive. He wanted to know her thoughts, her hopes and dreams, and what she loved and feared most.

He wanted to be the one to take her son fishing, although he had never baited a hook in his life. Being royal came with its own rules, and one of them was no hunting or fishing. Activities other people took for granted became cause for criticism when the royals did them, but he still wanted to take her son fishing.

He imagined the astonishment on Jeffrey's face when he caught his first fish, and the radiant happiness her son's joy would bring to Kirsten. He wanted to be part of the little family.

His pacing slowed as he thought about the boy.

Most children were awed by Rowe's royal background or his fame as a former champion racing-car driver, but Jeffrey didn't seem affected. The friendliness between them felt natural and right. Jeffrey was everything Rowe would have wanted in a son of his own. The father-son image came too easily, lingered too long in his mind.

What had happened to his vow to keep relationships strictly physical? Kirsten had happened, he acknowledged. Like her son, she didn't give a damn about his title, and she certainly wasn't angling to become a viscountess. She seemed content with her life as it was.

Did he have the right to turn that upside down? He knew what would happen if he pursued an involvement with her. He hadn't missed the looks they got when he turned up at the Castle School. Next would come the headlines linking them together. Within a couple of weeks, the media would have them all but married off.

So why didn't he get the heck out of here before she caught him hanging around her house like a love-sick teenager? She didn't need the headlines, and he didn't need the complication.

"Rowe, what are you doing here?"

At the sight of her, his heart thumped. She was so much more vibrant than his thoughts could capture. "You've done something to your hair," he said.

She touched it self-consciously. "I changed the color slightly."

It was all he could do to keep from threading his fingers through the gleaming strands. "You look beautiful."

She flushed. "Thanks. Was there something you wanted?"

You, he thought. Out loud he said, "I was working, and a couple of questions came up."

"They couldn't wait until Monday?"

He shouldn't have come. She didn't want him here. She had her arms full of packages, probably food she intended to prepare for the date she was expecting any minute. As his overactive imagination raced ahead, he didn't like where his thoughts were leading. "You're right, they'll keep," he grated. He stepped off the porch, willing himself not to react as his arm brushed hers in passing. "I'll see you in the office on Monday."

"Rowe," she said suddenly, halting his progress, "Why don't you come inside?"

Chapter Eight

He watched her move around the kitchen with the ease and grace of a dancer. She gestured toward two stools pulled up to a breakfast bar. "Have a seat. Would you like coffee or tea?"

Say no, invent some question she could answer, then leave, he ordered himself. He couldn't seem to make his legs obey. Accustomed to being in command of any situation, he felt shaken at how completely she had gained the upper hand, even if she didn't know it. "Coffee, thanks."

She opened a cupboard door. "How do you like it?"

"Black, one sugar, same as yours."

She frowned. "How do you know how I like my coffee?" In the office, one of the staff usually made it for them.

He hooked a leg over a stool, keeping the other leg on the floor, remembering the first time he had made coffee for her, remembering carrying it to a sleeping beauty he had woken in the time-honored way. The memory triggered a tidal wave of desire he had to struggle to control. "Two words—new shoes."

Kirsten frowned as the recollection rushed back. He meant the day she had foolishly worn a new pair of high heels to work and barely been able to walk home. She had fallen asleep in a chair and dreamed that he had kissed her. Striving to sound more offhand than she felt, she said, "Oh, that."

"Do you still wear them?"

"Not since the day you arrived. Too uncomfortable." Not only the shoes, but the reminder of her first encounter with him, she thought. He had worn an impeccably tailored business suit then. Now, in jeans and a checked shirt, he looked even more attractive. Suddenly, inviting him in seemed like playing with fire. It wouldn't help her keep their relationship on a business footing, and she didn't want anything else, did she?

He had looked lost waiting on her front porch, she decided. The curl falling onto his forehead reminded her so much of Jeffrey that he wakened all her mothering instincts.

"More flying pig?" she imagined Shara asking. All right, so the way Kirsten felt seeing him on her doorstep was a long way from motherly. It didn't mean she had to give in to it. Hadn't she learned anything from her sister's experience?

She made the coffee, welcoming the diversion while she got her tumultuous thoughts in order. They would have coffee, resolve whatever problem had brought him to her door, then she would let him leave.

She picked up her cup. "We'll be more comfortable in the living room."

He inspected the samples of Jeffrey's art covering the refrigerator, the effect cozy and familiar. "I'm comfortable right here."

She wasn't. Sharing the breakfast bar with Jeffrey was one thing, but touching thighs with Rowe in the limited space was quite another. She remained standing and sipped her coffee, wincing as it burned her tongue. "What do you want to see me about?"

He glanced at the empty stool beside him, as if well aware of what was in her mind. "I could make something up, but the truth is, I couldn't get much work done for thinking about you."

If it was a line, it sounded awfully convincing, she thought, abandoning her coffee to let it cool. Her tongue felt raw, not unlike her emotions. "You managed well enough yesterday. You hardly noticed when I left."

He put down his cup too, his dark gaze settling on her with disturbing effect. "I tried to convince myself of that, too. But I was aware of every move you made, from the rustle of your skirt as you walked back to your office to the swish of your hair as you brushed it before leaving. Did you know you have a habit of releasing a little breath of satisfaction just before you close your office door?"

She felt heat travel up her neck and into her face. "You're very observant," she said, hearing tension vibrate in her voice.

"I notice everything about you, Kirsten. Even things I don't want to notice. Like the way you frown when I intrude on anything remotely personal."

As he was about to do now, she thought, making an effort to keep her expression blank. "We don't have that kind of relationship." He had kissed her and she had responded, but that was all there was to it.

"Yet," he said quietly.

"Ever," she insisted. "I don't want to get involved with a man like..." Aware she had nearly said too much, she trailed off.

He rose and moved to within a hand span of where she stood with legs braced and fists clenched. "You were going to say, a man like me, weren't you? What is that supposed to mean?"

She willed herself not to step back. "Your image as a playboy who loves and leaves women is well-known."

"What if I told you it's only an image?"

She wouldn't believe him. Natalie's experience was more damning than anything he could say in his defense. "I'd wonder why you were trying so hard to convince me," she said in a tone barely above a whisper.

He touched the back of his hand to her cheek. "Do you really have to ask?"

Heat pooled on her skin where he touched. "This isn't a good idea."

"It's the best idea I've had in a long time." He took her hand. "Come with me now."

"Where?"

"You'll see." He looked at the packages she'd piled on the breakfast bar. "Unless you're expecting someone."

"No one," she admitted. "They're not ingredients for a dinner party. I went shopping."

He looked so relieved that she wondered what he thought she'd say. That she was expecting a man? A tremor shook her. Surely he wasn't jealous?

"Can I look?"

She wished he wouldn't, but he was already delving into the first carrier, grinning from ear to ear as he retrieved the lacy teddy she'd splurged on. The fragment of coffee-colored silk spilled from his hand. "Care to model this for me?"

She snatched it from him and thrust it back into the bag. "No."

Flirting was second nature with him. Stupid to let her heart speed up and her palms film with moisture when he probably only meant to show her something back at the office.

He clutched a hand to his heart as if wounded. "Then we're back to Plan A." With a regretful-sounding sigh, he dropped the teddy into the bag. "Finish your coffee and let's go."

Her suspicion seemed confirmed when he led her toward the executive suites. Instead of stopping there, he bounded up the steps leading to the round tower. Sketching the guard a salute, he escorted her through a pair of massive, metal-studded doors.

Her misgivings increased when she saw the guard suppress a smile. As far as she knew, the tower contained only galleries, reception rooms and a helipad on the roof. Oh, no, surely not.

"Wait a minute," she said, but he was already punching buttons on the incongruously modern elevator concealed behind a stone facade.

"No time."

They emerged onto a rooftop courtyard. In the middle of a painted circle sat a cream-colored helicopter streaked with red and blue, the royal crest adorning its side. Above them, the Carramer flag snapped in the breeze.

"No time for what?" she asked as he hurried her toward the helicopter.

"You'll soon see." He opened a door and helped her into the front passenger seat. Over her shoulder she glimpsed a cabin with leather-covered seats and brushed-gold fixtures. She had ridden in a helicopter before, but never one as luxurious as this. Rowe took the pilot's seat and handed her a set of headphones.

She adjusted them over her ears, wondering what on earth she was doing. She had no idea where Rowe planned to take her, or if she wanted to go. So why didn't she release the seat belt and climb out? Curiosity? Or a burning desire to spend time with him?

Both, she decided, wondering if she'd lost her mind. She knew what he was like. She had Jeffrey to consider. Letting a purely chemical reaction rule her actions made no sense at all. She stayed in her seat.

Vibration throbbed through her as the rotors made lazy circuits in the air. Through the headphones she heard Rowe talking to someone, although the exchange of pilot-speak meant little to her.

Then they lifted off. The tower dropped swiftly away, the people securing the castle for the evening becoming smudges against the green lawns and cobbled terraces. She had time to locate her house beside the village green and spot a herd of sun deer swarming into the sanctuary of home park, away from the helicopter sound. Minutes later the emerald expanse of the Pacific Ocean lay beneath them.

Her stomach lurched, the magnitude of what she was doing swamping her. Out here, they were truly alone.

An island appeared beneath them and she studied it to still her racing heart. A lagoon ringed with small rock islets curved around one side. Darker water suggested increased depth on the other. As the land rushed up to meet them, she glimpsed an interior crowded with avocado and mango trees, coconut palms and tropical hardwoods.

With the gentlest bump, he set the chopper down on a swath of hard-packed white sand, well above where strands of seaweed indicated the high-water mark. Removing the headphones, he turned to her. "Welcome to Jewel Cay, my island."

She handed him her headphones. "Your island?"

He exited the helicopter and moved around to her side. "Inherited along with the Aragon title," he said as he helped her down onto the sand.

She tried not to notice the feel of his hands spanning her waist. "And you brought me here because?"

He ducked her under the slowing rotors, straightening once they were clear. "I wanted to show you the sunset. Look."

With an arm around her shoulder, he turned her toward the west. He kept the arm there so that her attention was torn between the beauty of the sky rapidly flooding with orange and red, and the skittering of her heart.

The fireball sun seemed to be inside her, warming her from within, so it was hard to pay attention to anything else. Carramer was famous for its magnificent sunsets, and on Jewel Cay, she had never seen anything more spectacular. If not for the awareness of the man at her side, she would have been in awe of such splendor.

"Have you ever seen anything so lovely?" he asked.

His attention wasn't on the sunset, either, she discovered when she turned her head to find his heated gaze on her. She had been crazy to come with him. He was only interested in a physical relationship, and she had always promised herself she would wait for something deeper and more lasting.

She was swamped with so many sensations she felt dizzy. Was this what true desire felt like? For the first time Kirsten could understand how such a need could make one abandon the rules of a lifetime to follow where these wild and oh-so-compelling feelings might lead.

Even without experience to guide her, she recognized that she wanted him. Against all common sense, all she had heard about him, she wanted him to hold and touch her, wanted his mouth to ravage hers, silencing the nagging voice counseling her against such recklessness.

She should listen to that voice, recall her experiences of growing up with a father who was glamorous and exciting, but cared for no one but himself. His affairs, his inadequacy as a father, had taught her to rely on her own resources. She didn't want to feel such need for a man who would let her down the way her father had.

If more convincing was necessary, she had only to remember Rowe's silence when Jeffrey was born. Kirsten was proud of the life she had made for a child she loved with as much intensity as if she'd borne him herself. Where had Rowe been then?

He caressed the back of her neck, sending shivers down her spine. She didn't resist when he slid the hand across her shoulder and pulled her against him. She fought to hold on to common sense, the feelings were so strong. She rested her head into the curve of his neck, breathing in the heady fragrance of salty sea air on his skin, and pure maleness. Her pulse quickened.

What was she supposed to *do* with these feelings? She didn't want them but couldn't seem to fight his effect on her. Didn't want to, if truth be told. What she really wanted was to press closer against him, ever closer, until the mystery of the ultimate union of man and woman was a mystery to her no longer.

Shocked at where her thoughts were leading, she tried to move away, but he held her too tightly. "It's all right, I won't hurt you," he murmured, brushing her windblown hair back off her face with his free hand.

He'd already hurt her far more than he could ever imagine. The probability that he could do it again was real. He could love her and leave her, as he was notorious for doing. That would be terrible enough. Far worse, he could hurt her child, and that she simply wouldn't allow.

She found the strength to step away, and this time he didn't restrain her. "I didn't mean to move so fast," he said. "You have a devastating effect on me."

The feeling was definitely mutual, but she kept silent.

He raked long fingers through his hair. "Say something, Kirsten, anything."

"I'd like to go back to Merrisand."

"Right now?"

If she said yes, would he comply? She never found out, because he closed the distance between them and took her in his arms again. Her back was against a sandstone outcrop, the stone smooth and sun-warmed.

She felt the heat from the rock warm her as he pressed her against it, or was it her incendiary response to his nearness?

She only knew that when he bent his head, his intention unmistakable, her resistance vanished as if it had never existed. Almost of their own accord her arms linked around his neck, and her lips parted in invitation.

He took his time, the anticipation building inside her until she feared if he didn't kiss her soon, she would explode. Still his mouth hovered over hers, tantalizingly near but not touching. Not yet.

The waiting was agony, but was as nothing compared to the pleasure that spiraled through her when he kissed the corner of her mouth, his tongue caressing the sensitized area. This wasn't a kiss; this was a dance of desire such as she'd never had before.

Her breath escaped on a sigh of wonder and impatience. She strained against him, trying to capture his mouth completely, but he put a heartbeat of distance between them, his smile telling her he knew perfectly well what he was doing to her.

She couldn't help herself. She touched her tongue to the place where he had kissed her so lightly. The moment she did, he crushed her mouth with a kiss that drove everything but pleasure out of her mind.

It was difficult to remember why she shouldn't be here, to remember anything except how wonderful his mouth tasted, how hard and lean his body felt. She clung to him, hypoxia making her light-headed but not caring. She needed this more than she needed air to breathe.

After the deepest kiss she'd ever experienced, she stirred in protest as he drew away. She didn't want this to end, ever. Threading his fingers through her hair, he gently pulled her head back, covering her exposed throat with kisses, lingering longest over the wildly skittering pulse betraying her true state of mind.

Forcing her eyes open, she was stunned to see flames leaping in his gaze. All the sensation wasn't on her side. He felt it, too. Her spirits soared as she realized she had put the flames there. She had power over him, as well.

"Do you still want to go back to Merrisand?" he growled.

"Yes." She could hardly force the word out but was proud of managing it, anyway. She wasn't entirely under his spell. How close she was, she refused to think.

"But not right this minute?"

Why did he have to make this so hard? If only he would get into the helicopter again and fly them back to the castle, she'd be able to overcome the desire coursing through her. She should have the strength to insist, to climb back aboard the chopper with or without him, waiting inside for as long as it took to make the point that she wasn't his for the taking.

What was she waiting for?

"We'll go back after I've shown you my island," he said when she remained silent.

Telling herself that a sightseeing tour wouldn't hurt, she nodded, every part of her shimmering with long-suppressed needs. Perhaps walking would help her regain some control. Heaven knew, she had little enough at this moment. He had only to lower her to the pristine sand and she would have been his.

With a last, faintly guilty glance at the helicopter,

she accompanied him along a path made of lustrous coral.

From the air, the island had looked uninhabited. Hidden in the rain forest was a cabin, more a cabana, really. The roof was thatched and the woven walls didn't reach all the way to the ground. Inside, the floor was tiled and the furniture was made of bamboo.

She averted her eyes from a large platform bed occupying one end of the one-roomed dwelling, noting comfortable armchairs, a bookshelf filled with books and topped with a cluster of candles.

A modern kitchen was divided from the living area by a bamboo-clad breakfast bar. She started when Rowe snapped on an electric light; she'd expected him to light the candles. They would have been kinder, revealed less of her aroused state, she thought.

"I'm not Robinson Crusoe," he said, seeing her reaction. "I have a tropical-fruit plantation on the other side of the island, managed by a couple. They keep the cabana stocked for my visits."

Her skin was so sensitized, she felt she might jump out of it if he touched her. Say something, anything, she commanded herself despite her dry throat. "Do you spend a lot of time here?"

He moved into the kitchen and got out glasses, pouring amber-colored juice into them from a refrigerator under the breakfast bar. "This is my retreat from the world. I come as often as I can get away, which isn't nearly as often as I'd like."

And he had brought her here. She drank the juice, welcoming the bittersweet taste. "What is this?"

"Pineapple guava from fruit grown on the plantation. Like it?"

"It's very different. Quite good."

"You don't sound too sure."

She wasn't sure, not about any of this. She was angry with him for being who he was and having power over her, anyway. Angry with herself for not having the strength to insist on returning to the castle. Wanting him more than she'd ever wanted anything. Hating herself for wanting him.

For the first time Kirsten felt a glimmer of understanding about her mother. How much in love she must have been to take her father back time after time, despite his affairs and his capriciousness. Kirsten had always assumed it was because of Natalie and her.

Now she wondered: was this how her mother had felt about her father?

She hadn't heard Rowe move to her side until his fingers brushed hers as he removed the glass. A great shudder shook her. When he opened his arms, she went into them unresistingly, a lemming who could do nothing else.

"You feel good here," he said.

In the cabin or in his arms? Both felt much better to her than they should.

"I don't bring many people here," he answered her unspoken question. "But you don't feel like an outsider. You feel like part of me. How has that happened so fast?"

She rested her forehead against his shoulder. "I don't know."

He caught her chin, gently forcing her to look at him. "You feel it, too, don't you?"

She felt color bloom on her cheeks, a betrayal in itself. No matter how often she told herself she shouldn't feel this way, she couldn't stem the tidal wave of desire sweeping through her as she met his hungry gaze. "Yes."

"Then it can't be anything but right. I'll make it good for us both, trust me."

Two words, so innocent yet so dangerous. Yet on some level, she did trust him, at least in this. The needs, the wants, the yearning were so strong that she clung to him, afraid that whatever he wanted from her, she would give him, regardless of the rights and wrongs of it. From the moment she met Rowe, the word *no* seemed to have been erased from her vocabulary.

But what came after *yes?* It looked very much as if she was to find out.

Chapter Nine

First he brought out champagne. One well-known to be a superb vintage, she noticed with the heightened awareness she seemed to have around him. He opened it expertly with a sigh more than a pop, and poured the golden nectar into cut-crystal goblets.

There was a bell-like sound as he touched his glass to hers. "To a night out of time."

"A night out of time."

As she echoed the toast, she thought how true it was. Tonight she wasn't Natalie's sister or Jeffrey's mother. She was a woman on the verge of discovering love for the first time. The idea might seem foolish these days. She had been teased about her virgin state often enough by Natalie, who had boasted that Rowe hadn't been her first or only lover. Kirsten might have doubted he was Jeffrey's father, if not for the strong resemblance between them.

Rowe leaned over and kissed her, his tongue lapping at the wetness there. "You taste of champagne."

"So do you."

"Like it?"

"I've never tasted second-hand champagne before."

He grimaced. "Spoken like a true romantic."

She put the glass down before her shaking hand betrayed how new she was at this. "I haven't had much experience at this kind of thing."

Understatement of the year.

He nodded. "I can understand you feeling overwhelmed by the helicopter and the island. Hopefully not by me."

Him most of all.

"Would you like something to eat?"

Lunch with Shara had been hours ago, but Kirsten wasn't really hungry. She said yes, anyway, hoping the ordinary activity would defuse some of the intensity of the moment.

He delved into the refrigerator again. "Good, Jill hasn't let me down."

"Jill?"

"One of the caretakers I mentioned who provision the cabin for me when I let them know I'm coming."

He brought out a leaf-shaped platter beautifully arranged with a variety of cheeses and tropical fruits. Selecting a sliver of mango, he offered it to her. As her mouth closed around the succulent piece, she knew there could be nothing ordinary about anything Rowe did.

Sweet and moist, the morsel of fruit slid down her throat. When he gathered up an escaped drop of juice from her chin with one finger, she felt giddy. His gaze on her burned as he licked the juice from his fingertip.

Dear Lord, he could make any activity into a sensual experience.

"More?"

She couldn't speak for the tension clogging her throat, so she nodded. He cut a piece of soft cheese studded with apricots and placed it on a round of bread. When he lifted it to her mouth, she intercepted him. "I can manage, thanks." If he kept feeding her so provocatively, she couldn't answer for the consequences.

He gave her the food, then cut some fruit and cheese for himself. Watching him eat was almost as arousing, yet she couldn't make herself look away. By the time the light meal was finished, her body felt on fire.

"Would you like to go for a swim?"

Had he read her mind? Plunging into the sea would at least put out some of the flames. But it was almost dark. "Now?"

"The moon will be up soon. The lagoon is safe. The reef keeps sharks out."

The most alarming predator was the one right in front of her. She hadn't even considered sharks. "I didn't bring anything with me. I can hardly swim in my underwear."

"Why not? There's no one to see you and you'll be up to your neck in water."

She was already in over her head. How much worse could the ocean be?

Snagging an armful of towels from a shelf, he led the way back along the coral path, past the helicopter to a crescent of sand gleaming whitely against the darkening sky. Phosphorescent tips capped the waves gently lapping the sand.

The rising moon provided just enough light for her to undress by, and not so much that she felt shy about Rowe seeing her in so little. Her bra and panties were a rich plum color, the figure-hugging silk garments flattering a shape she had worked hard to maintain. Perhaps not the equal of the models he'd been photographed alongside, but nothing to be ashamed of, either.

Ready to plunge into the waves, she looked up as he shed the last of his clothes. Moonlight silvered his magnificent body, highlighting every muscular contour. He stepped out of his jeans and stood resplendent in black shorts that did more to emphasize his masculinity than nudity would have done.

Her heart almost stopped. He had been ready to make love to her at the cabin, suggesting the meal and a swim to relax her, she suspected. Suddenly she didn't want a swim. She wanted him. Her mouth went dry again and her pulse raced. What would he say if she offered herself to him now, on the beach?

She wasn't given a chance. He padded silently over the sand and walked into the water until he was hip-deep, then executed a shallow dive like an arrow arcing through the air. Entering the water with hardly a splash, he began to cleave powerful strokes across the waves, parallel with the beach.

He was beautiful to watch. She could have happily stood there all night absorbing the poetry of his movements. If her heart wasn't pounding and her breathing ragged with the need to be close to him. If he hadn't suddenly reared out of the water closer than she expected him to be, and lifted her against his water-slick chest.

His cold wet touch shrilled through her and she

kicked out, every sense on instant alert. "What are you doing?"

"Not swimming alone."

"Put me down."

"As you wish."

Too late she realized what she had invited. Her furious kicks made no impact and he silenced her objections by the simple expedient of kissing her again. Shivering with cold, she felt heat sear her at the touch of mouth to mouth. How could she feel both hot and cold at the same time?

He lifted his head, his intention clear. She linked her arms around his neck and hung on. "Please, you can't..."

He could. He did. Holding her tightly against him, he waded back into the water.

"You told me to put you down." She tried to brace herself, but the sudden plunge into coldness when he released her made her loosen her grip on him. She gasped as the water closed over her.

Then she was scooped up in his arms again, being kissed as she had never been kissed before. She knew she would never taste salt again without thinking of this moment. "You rat, why did you dunk me?" she demanded through chattering teeth when he let her come up for air.

Moonlight glinted off his smile. "Have you any notion of how fantastic silk looks when it gets wet?"

She glanced down. She may as well have been naked, her nipples standing out in hard nubs against her sodden bra. Her chest heaved, adding to the effect. "I thought you wanted to swim," she said, her voice hoarse with tension.

"A few minutes ago I thought so, too."

"And now?"

Without answering, he carried her back to the sand and kicked open one of the towels, then set her down on it, retrieving the other to place behind her head. She could hardly breathe as he knelt beside her. "This is what I feel like doing."

His words sounded as labored as her breathing. She sucked in a strangled breath at the touch of his hands skimming over her body, over the wet mounds of her breasts and down her sides. Her slick skin offered little resistance and she felt goose bumps develop everywhere he touched. Not with cold this time, but with the wondrously erotic sensations he created.

Her hands crept up to link around his neck, and she pulled his face down until she could taste her fill of his marvelous mouth. Salt had become her favorite flavor. She couldn't get enough of it. Of him.

He became tense suddenly, and reached to untangle her hands from his neck. "What is it?" she asked. Had she done something wrong out of inexperience?

Even his silence sounded strained. "We can't do this."

"You don't want to make love to me?" She couldn't help it. Hurt trembled in her voice.

"I've wanted to from the moment I saw you leading that tour group at the castle. Since we couldn't very well make love with your son in the house, I've had to take a lot of cold showers waiting for this moment."

The thought that wanting her had driven him to distraction was deliciously satisfying. "Then what's the matter?"

"When we left the cabin, all I brought with me were the towels."

He still wasn't making sense. "What else do we need?"

In the moonlight, his face seemed made of granite. Only his fiery gaze told her this wasn't rejection. He carved a hand through his hair, leaving trails. "Are you on the pill?" he asked.

"No, of course not. I've had no need." The words had barely left her mouth when light dawned and she scrambled to sit up. How stupid could one woman be? He meant he hadn't brought any *protection* with him. And it hadn't crossed her mind because she hadn't meant to let things go this far.

"Because there's been no man in your life since Jeffrey's father?" he asked. She was tempted to let him think it was the reason. He must have read the dilemma in her expression because he said, "There's something else, isn't there. Are you trying to tell me you can't have more children?"

"No. I mean, I don't know."

He swung around to face her. "Was Jeffrey conceived in violence? Is that the problem? You can tell me, Kirsten. I won't think any less of you, I promise. I need to know, to understand what's going on with you."

Hearing his voice roughen with concern, knowing it was for her, was almost her undoing. "I don't want to discuss it," she said, wishing she had resisted him, then he wouldn't be asking questions she couldn't answer.

Rowe touched a hand to her cheek. "If you conceived Jeffrey as a result of an attack, you must know it wasn't your fault. You have nothing to be ashamed of."

Her control reached snapping point and she jerked

her head away. "You have no idea what you're talking about."

"Then tell me. At least tell me where I can find the son of a...the man who fathered your child, then didn't stick around, so I can make him regret the day he was born."

"You don't have to look far."

The words were out before she could bite them back. Horrified, she sprang to her feet. "I'll get dressed and you can take me back to Merrisand."

He moved like lightning, looming over her so that she shrank away involuntarily. "Not so fast. First you're going to explain a few things."

"There's nothing to explain. I'm sure you can work it out for yourself."

His hands clamped over her arms. "I thought I had, but I wasn't even close, was I? If I didn't know better, I'd think you were trying to tell me you're a virgin."

She closed her eyes to veil her answer, but she couldn't hide the shudders rippling through her. Embarrassment made her face so hot that even in the low light he noticed.

His next words confirmed it. "My Lord, you are."

Even now, when the risk of discovery loomed over her, she could still be distracted by the hot, wild yearnings gripping her as she collided with him. Not wanting to own the feelings, she tried to twist free, but he caught her hands and pinned them behind her back.

"Not until you tell me how a virgin can have a child."

She turned her head aside. "I don't have to explain anything to you."

"Not long ago I'd have agreed, but we've come too far. I'm entitled to know what's going on."

The break she heard in his voice was like a knife in her heart. Was it right to keep the truth from him any longer? And was she tempted to tell him for Jeffrey's sake, or her own? Not sure of the answer, she kept silent.

Rowe filled it for her. "Did you tell Jeffrey's father that he has a son?"

She nodded. This she could answer, "He didn't want to know."

Rowe swore softly. "If he was mine, I'd move heaven and earth to be part of his life."

Suddenly he stilled, his expression darkening. "At least I would if I was given the chance."

"What do you mean?" she asked, terrified that she already knew.

"Let's start with the uncanny resemblance between Jeffrey and me."

"Coincidence," she tried desperately.

"Or genetics. He looks more like me than he does you. From the first time I met him I sensed a bond between us that defies explanation. As crazy and impossible as it seems, could I be his father?"

The truth burst from her in a sob. "Yes. Damn you. Yes."

He looked thunderstruck, as if he had expected another denial and could barely absorb what she'd said. "It's true then. I'm a father. I have a son."

Then his expression hardened again. "This doesn't make sense. How could we have made love without me remembering every moment?"

Thinking of the harm he'd done to her sister, she shuddered. "It wouldn't be the first time."

"What in the blazes is that supposed to mean?"

She lifted her head. "Isn't your specialty loving women and leaving them?"

"Just because the media write what they like and royal protocol doesn't allow me to defend myself, doesn't make it true."

"So you're not the Lothario you're made out to be, but a misunderstood knight in shining armor?"

Her sarcasm, fueled by desperation, reached its target. "You tempt me to live up to my image more than any woman I've ever met. But I won't be side-tracked this time. I'm still dealing with the fact that Jeffery is my son. That usually means his mother and I had to have slept together. If we had, I'd remember every touch, every breath. And I'd make darned sure you remembered, too. Yet you admit this is the first time any man ever tried to make love to you. What the devil is going on?"

All it took was for his hold to slip momentarily and she was sprinting away, driven as much by her own demons as by the need to avoid giving him the answers he demanded. She hadn't believed herself capable of such primitive responses as he dragged from her. She hadn't put up so much as a shred of resistance. Even now, running away from him across the beach, she ached to turn and throw herself into his arms.

Shame warred with pleasure inside her. What sort of man was he to command her body so, when her mind knew him for what he was? He had said his image was a media fiction, but that didn't explain Natalie's experience.

Sobs of rage and remorse burst from her as she ran. She had no idea where she was going, only that she needed to put as much distance between them as she could.

"Kirsten, stop!"

She heard his footsteps behind her and ran faster. Tears blinded her, and so she didn't see the rocks half-buried in sand until she stumbled over them. A tangle of seaweed snared her foot and she felt herself falling. Shock jolted along the arms she extended to save herself, then a moment of blinding light and the moonlight was eclipsed by blackness.

Rowe saw her stumble, get tangled in the seaweed, put out her hands to save herself and fall heavily, her head striking a rock.

Reaching her, he swore using words he'd learned as a boy from the palace guards who hadn't known he was listening.

He turned her over gently, exercising his vocabulary anew at the nasty cut marring her forehead. She moaned softly but didn't rouse as he flushed the gash with seawater. The wound looked deep, but it was clean. He checked her carefully but didn't find any signs of broken bones. Safe to move her, then. He scooped her up into his arms.

All hell was going to break loose if he arrived back at Merrisand with an injured woman, the two of them dressed only in their underwear. But she needed help, and he couldn't risk dressing her in case he caused her more harm. All hell would have to break loose, then. He'd ridden out worse.

He was pretty sure she hadn't, though, as he lifted her carefully aboard the chopper and placed her along a row of seats. He pulled pillows and blankets from an overhead compartment, and he covered her before crisscrossing a web of seat belts over her body. Her wound was bleeding, and she looked terrifyingly slight and pale, she hadn't denied his assertion that she was a virgin. Yet she was the mother of his child. When he'd demanded answers, she'd run like a rabbit.

None of this made sense.

He snared a first-aid kit from another compartment and dressed Kirsten's wound. The first pad quickly became saturated with blood, so he replaced it with another that stayed a little drier, giving him hope that he had stemmed the bleeding for the moment. The sooner he got her back to the castle, the better.

Wishing he could split himself in two and stay beside her, as well as fly the chopper, he had to force himself into the pilot's seat where he made a radio call arranging to have the royal physician, Alain Pascale, meet the helicopter. Usually Pascale was based in Solano, and Rowe was thankful that he was visiting the castle at present. He might be a crusty old curmudgeon who would have plenty to say when Rowe arrived with his patient, but he was the best doctor in Carramer, and also the most discreet.

His hands busy on the controls, Rowe's mind worked overtime. If he had ever patronized a sperm bank, he would have an explanation, but royalty simply didn't do that sort of thing. Too much risk to the line of succession. So how did he come to have a son, and how did Kirsten fit into the picture?

Maybe she'd worked for a medical laboratory and stolen his sperm after he'd had a checkup. It would explain how she could have his child when they had never made love.

There was one other possibility, he thought, banking the chopper as the lights of Merrisand came into view. She wasn't Jeffrey's mother at all.

So obvious. Why hadn't he thought of it before? Her effect on him had snarled his thinking, preventing him from putting two and two together until now. He wrenched the joystick and almost sent the chopper into a spin until he wrestled it level again. That had to be the answer. Somehow, somewhere, Rowe had slept with Jeffrey's real mother, fathering the child that Kirsten now regarded as her own.

He glanced over his shoulder. She was still unconscious and moving restively against the restraints. He felt like a brute. She'd been harmed because of him, and he would move heaven and earth to put things right. Both her present injuries and her single-parent status. If he was right and she had raised his son as her own, Rowe owed her a great debt, and he believed in paying his debts.

His body's instinctive response caught him unawares. If he was right and she was a virgin… Rowe felt choked thinking about it, and knew that, whatever else was between them, he wanted to be the first man for her. To take her places she'd never dreamed of going, soar with her on winds of desire. First he had to get her well, then he needed answers. After that…

He made himself concentrate on flying. The landing pad on top of the round tower was floodlit, and Dr. Pascale and a trauma team clambered into the chopper before the rotors stopped turning. The doctor's examination was punctuated by Rowe's cursory explanation of the accident.

Bending over Kirsten, the doctor asked, "How long has she been unconscious?"

"No more than fifteen minutes."

Pascale turned to a nurse. "Looks like a grade-three concussion. I want her admitted to the castle infirmary for an MRI scan and hourly observation."

"Will she be all right?"

The doctor looked at Rowe as if he'd temporarily forgotten the viscount's existence. "I'm a doctor, not a fortune-teller, but concussion isn't usually life-threatening, provided there's no edema, hemorrhaging or other brain injury."

The nurse spoke up. "Doctor, she's coming around."

Rowe was happy to have the doctor forget him again and turn his attention to Kirsten, getting her to recite the months of the year backward and tell him the day and date. Rowe assumed Pascale was establishing the extent of her injury. Pascale seemed satisfied by her answers and ordered his team to put Kirsten on a stretcher and take her to the infirmary.

"Set up the MRI. I'll be right there."

Rowe was ready to follow, but the doctor forestalled him. "That's hardly the uniform of the day, Viscount Aragon."

In his concern for Kirsten, Rowe had forgotten his state of undress. In his haste to get help for Kirsten, he had left their clothes back on the island. "You can lend me a white coat at the infirmary."

The doctor closed his bag and climbed out of the chopper, gesturing for Rowe to follow. "Mind telling me what happened? Beyond the basics this time."

"Yes, I do mind. For the record we were taking a moonlight swim. She fell on a slippery rock and hit her head."

"And off the record?"

Rowe scrubbed a hand across his chin. "We had an argument. She was running away from me."

Instead of berating him, the doctor surprised Rowe by clasping his shoulder. "So you finally found out about Jeffrey. When Prince Maxim told me you and Kirsten were working together, I wondered how long it would take you."

Chapter Ten

Rowe stared at the doctor. "What are you saying?"

"Last time I was at Merrisand, I met Kirsten and her child at a picnic for the castle staff. Seeing young Jeffrey was like looking at a picture of you at the same age. You're his father, aren't you?"

Rowe's brisk pace faltered. "Does anybody else know?"

"I doubt it. Even if they noticed the likeness, they'd write it off as coincidence. They don't know your family as well as I do. Over three decades of ministering to royal patients gives me something of an edge."

Rowe knew his expression was bleak. "Where were you a couple of weeks ago when I first met Kirsten?"

"Growing orchids at my estate in Solano. I wouldn't be here now if I hadn't been attending a growers' convention in Taures and decided to drop in on Maxim and Giselle between sessions. You mean, you didn't find out about your relationship with the boy until today?''

Rowe shook his head. "I saw the resemblance right away and I felt a connection I couldn't explain, but Kirsten and I had never been involved."

"That you can remember."

Rowe almost groaned aloud. "Not you, too."

"Serves you right for not settling down with the right woman and doing your royal duty providing heirs to the throne."

"I leave that to my cousins. It's not that easy finding the right woman."

"Until now." Before Rowe could argue, the doctor said, "When I came aboard, your expression told me all I needed to know. You're in love with her, aren't you."

Was he? Rowe wasn't sure he knew what love was. Certainly he was more attracted to Kirsten than to any woman he'd ever known. He was surprised how much he wanted to take care of her and Jeffrey. Fine job he'd made of it tonight.

"Come on," the doctor urged. "No need to settle the succession right now. First we have to get that little lady fixed up. According to Prince Maxim, she's a pearl."

Rowe and Maxim might have different grounds for regarding Kirsten as a pearl—at least Rowe hoped they did, otherwise he might have to flatten his bachelor cousin—but Rowe couldn't argue with the conclusion.

She *was* a pearl, beautiful and rare. Murderous rage welled in him at the thought of her lying injured, an injury he had caused, however inadvertently. "Will you keep her in the infirmary long?" he asked as the doctor led the way to the infirmary located at the western end of the state-apartment complex. Rowe studiously ignored the veiled curiosity of the guards. Hadn't they seen a viscount walk around the castle in his underwear before?

"Only overnight, then she can go home to rest, although she shouldn't be left alone for the next few days."

Rowe felt his mouth tighten. "She won't be. I'll have a suite prepared for her and Jeffrey next to mine. I'll take care of her myself."

"The gossipmongers will have a field day."

Rowe looked down at himself. "It's a bit late to worry now. This will be all over Merrisand by tomorrow."

The doctor chuckled. "A fake medical emergency to test the castle's response mechanism is newsworthy, but it's hardly front-page news."

The physician's eleventh-hour invention of a cover story for the mishap was inspired. "Thanks," he said simply.

"Don't mention it."

At the infirmary Pascale handed Rowe a white coat. It was stretched taut across his broad shoulders, but was a big improvement on the shorts he was wearing. When the doctor finally allowed Rowe to look in on Kirsten, his outfit earned him a dreamy smile. "Changed your profession?"

Seeing how delicate she looked in the luxurious room, he barely kept his dismay from showing. "They drummed me out of lifeguarding."

"Not on my account, I hope?"

He didn't like the sound of that. "How much do you remember about the accident?"

"I remember you suggesting a swim, but nothing afterward until I woke up in the helicopter. I must have hit my head on a submerged rock. Did you dive in and rescue me?"

He felt a twinge of guilt. He was going to have to tell her why she'd run from him, but not yet. Not sure which of them he was protecting, he said, "Something like that."

"Thank you." Her forehead creased.

"Are you in pain?" When she nodded he reached for the call button. The staff had discreetly given them some time alone, but the doctor should be here, giving Kirsten whatever she needed.

Kirsten winced. "I have the mother of all headaches, but Dr. Pascale said that's to be expected. Evidently it's also normal that I can't recall the time right before the accident. I'm glad I can remember your beautiful island."

"You'll see it again as soon as you're well," he promised. Next time he wouldn't drive her away from him. He would know the truth about her and his son, and they would be there together.

She stirred restively. Where the blazes was the doctor? "I'm okay," she assured him. "But I have to get out of here before Jeffrey gets home."

Rowe took her hand. How delicate her fingers felt curled in his. He shuddered as emotion curled through him in response. "You need to rest. I'll meet Jeffrey and bring him to see you."

"You don't have time to look after a six-year-old."

"I'll make time." For his son, he would make all the time in the world.

"Are you sure?"

She sounded so reluctant to impose on him that he

felt angry—until he reminded himself of her injury. Reluctant admiration surged through him. Had she always been so fiercely independent? Was that why she was determined to raise his child without asking for his help? Why the devil hadn't anyone told him about Jeffrey during the past six years? The doctor had suspected Jeffrey was his, but had left them to work out their own destiny. But Kirsten could have said something.

"I'm sure," he said, biting back everything else he wanted to say. This wasn't the time or the place. The questions tearing at him could wait a little longer.

Her sigh of capitulation wrenched at him. "Very well, but only until the doctor lets me out of here. My keys are in my purse."

Luckily she had left that in the chopper. A nurse bustled in at last. "I'm sorry to keep you waiting, Your Lordship. The doctor is going over Ms. Bond's MRI results."

Rowe tensed. "And?"

"Dr. Pascale will explain them to you. It's all good news," she said with a smile of reassurance. When Rowe told her about Kirsten's headache, the nurse adjusted a drip feeding into her patient's arm. "This will help."

About time, Rowe thought, managing to keep the words to himself. When had he become so sensitive to Kirsten's needs? It was more than discovering she had probably been raising his child. He cared about her for herself, as well.

He was glad to have the task of moving her and Jeffrey's things into a suite beside his own. It kept him from looking too closely at what it all might mean.

After the doctor assured him Kirsten's scan showed no lesions suggesting brain injury beyond the concussion, Rowe's mood lifted. "She needs complete rest until her symptoms clear, then she can gradually return to normal activities," the doctor added.

Thinking of how much worse the prognosis could have been, Rowe felt his knees turning to jelly. He quickly mastered the momentary weakness, but not in time for Pascale to miss it. "You should get some rest yourself," the doctor said.

"I will, as soon as I've taken care of Jeffrey." He could snatch a nap at her place while waiting for the neighbor to bring the little boy home from their fishing trip.

Pascale's eyes narrowed. "See that you do, or I'll have two patients on my hands, wrecking my orchid-growing conference completely."

Seeing the concern the doctor tried to mask, Rowe felt a surge of affection for the elderly physician who had delivered most of the present generation of royal children. Pascale may have married an Australian, but his heart belonged completely to Carramer and its ruling dynasty. It was amazing how often he managed to be there for one of the family during a crisis.

Rowe shook his hand. "Thanks for everything."

Pascale's other hand covered his. "You're welcome. My fee is the same as always—the right to deliver your children when the time comes."

Rowe wasn't sure of his feelings for Kirsten, but the thought of having children with her was surprisingly appealing. "Aren't you getting ahead of yourself?" he asked gruffly.

The doctor gave him a shrewdly assessing look. "You'd know better than me. Now get out of here and let me do my job so I can get back to my *Cymbidium carramerii.*''

Since there was nothing more he could do for Kirsten at the moment, Rowe complied. Despite his exhaustion, he needed activity. He returned to his apartment to shower and dress, then gritted his teeth and called his cousin. He didn't like waking Maxim, who sounded alarmed at the news until Rowe assured him Kirsten would be all right. By the time he got off the phone, he had the prince's blessing to make whatever arrangements he thought best. Maxim also agreed to go along with Pascale's cover story that the accident had been a drill to test the castle's emergency procedures.

Rowe started issuing orders. By the time day fully dawned, a suite was ready for Kirsten and Jeffrey next to his. All he could do was go to her cottage and wait.

He hadn't meant to do more than nap, but the night's events took their toll and he was asleep on her couch when he was wakened by the slamming of the front door. "Mommy, we're back."

Seeing Rowe stretched out on the sofa, the child screeched to a halt. "Hello."

Rowe swung himself upright. At the sight of Jeffrey, his breath caught. In a checked shirt pulling free of his jeans, the knees grass-stained, the child looked like a character out of a Mark Twain novel. How could Rowe not have recognized the relationship between them? It seemed so obvious now. Emotions he could barely identify made his voice thicken. "My name is Rowe, remember? Did you have a good fishing trip?"

Jeffrey pulled off his battered cloth hat adorned

with fishing flies and dropped it on a chair. "Yes, thank you. Michael's dad is bringing my fish in."

Rowe smiled. "Must be some catch if it needs a grown-up to carry it."

The child's face fell. "I lost a really big one. I saw it before it got off my hook, and it was this big." He held his small hands wide apart, making Rowe smile.

Rowe patted the seat beside him. "We need to talk, man to man."

Jeffrey looked uncertain. "Am I in trouble? Where's my mommy?"

"You're not in trouble, son." *Son.* A word Rowe had used without thinking as recently as yesterday. Now the meaning behind it made his throat swell and speech become nearly impossible. He coughed. "I have some news for you."

Jeffrey's eyes widened as he put two and two together. "Is something the matter with Mommy?"

"She's okay. She had a small accident and the doctor is taking care of her in the infirmary."

Jeffrey's mouth trembled and his small fists clenched, but he met Rowe's gaze unwaveringly. Rowe's mind spun back to when he'd been told about his father's disappearance. He'd been only a couple of years older than Jeffrey and had felt as if his world had shattered into little bits. He had also put on a brave face, insisting he was fine.

Inside he had been far from fine, but his mother had believed the act. Or wanted to. As a result he was denied the comfort he desperately needed but hadn't known how to ask for.

Rowe reached for the boy's hand. "You don't have to be brave. I won't tell your mother if you get a bit upset. It's a secret between us men."

The child's luminous eyes swam. "I don't want her to be hurt. I want her here."

Tugging on the hand in his, Rowe enfolded his son's small body in the bear hug he'd once wanted for himself. At the contact, he felt something break away inside, like pieces of an iceberg. The sensation intensified when Jeffrey buried his face against Rowe's chest. The small shoulders shook, but Rowe said nothing, waiting for the storm to pass.

After a few minutes Jeffrey sniffed hard and blew into the handkerchief Rowe held out to him. "How did Mommy get hurt?"

"We went swimming. She fell and hit her head on a rock, so when you see her she'll have a bandage on her forehead. Nothing to be scared about."

"Will she get better?"

"She's already better. The doctor only wants her to stay in hospital a little while so she can rest."

"Why can't she rest here?"

Rowe placed his hands on the child's shoulders. "She needs somebody to take care of her, just like she does for you when you're sick. How would you like to stay at the state apartments with her while she's resting?"

Jeffrey regarded him with suspicion. "What's a state 'partment?"

"The big building that looks like a castle on the way to your school."

"With the flag on top?"

"The same one."

"Will Mommy be there?"

Rowe shook his head. "Not yet. We'll go and see her in the infirmary, and you can ask the doctor when she can come to the apartment with us."

"Who will look after me till she gets there?"

"Have you ever stayed in the castle?"

"No, we live here."

"At the castle we have lots of servants, people whose job it is to look after us. They'll take care of both of us, and your mommy, too."

Jeffrey looked thoughtful. "If I tell them I want ice cream, will they get it for me?"

Rowe felt his mouth twitch but answered seriously, "They'll bring you all the ice cream you can eat."

"But no carrots?"

"Maybe a few. You don't grow strong enough to catch huge fish without eating carrots."

Jeffrey made a face. "At the camp last night Michael's daddy gave me stew with carrots in it. I threw them away into a bush. Is that why my fish got away?"

"No doubt about it." Rowe stood up. "Why don't we go and tell Michael's father what's happened, then pack up what you want to take to the apartment?"

"Can I play Doom Planet there?"

Cheered by the boy's resilience, Rowe smiled. "I'm sure we can arrange something." When the younger royals visited Merrisand, they enjoyed the same entertainments as any other children. There was bound to be a computer game set up somewhere. If it didn't have Doom Planet, Rowe would soon get it.

Kirsten's neighbors, Shara and Paul, were concerned at Rowe's news and promised to visit as soon as Kirsten was ready. Jeffrey needed convincing that his friend, Michael, couldn't move to the state apartments with them, but eventually Rowe got the child settled in. To Rowe it looked as if Jeffrey had brought along half the contents of his room, but he said nothing, sure that Jeffrey was more upset about his mother than he was letting on.

When they returned to the infirmary, Kirsten was awake. Her color looked better and the drip had been removed from her arm. Just as well, because Jeffrey hurtled himself at her.

Seeing her arms tighten around the child, Rowe felt a momentary pang of jealousy he quickly subdued. "How are you?"

Her gaze became haunted. "Dr. Pascale says I'll be fine after a few days' rest. I still don't remember the accident."

Jeffrey gently touched the dressing on her forehead. "Does it hurt?"

"Only a little. Seeing you is the best medicine."

The child snuggled closer. "Good. I don't want you to be sick."

She smiled. "That makes two of us." She regarded Rowe anxiously. "The doctor said you've moved us into the state apartments."

He nodded. "You can rest there, knowing Jeffrey's in good hands. The staff has had plenty of practice caring for royal children."

If she noticed his unconscious use of the term "royal children," she gave no sign. "I hate to put you to so much trouble. You have your hands full with the race."

"Forget the race." *He* had, he realized in some surprise. Ever since he'd taken her to the island, she'd occupied his thoughts to the exclusion of everything else.

At his vehemence she shrank back against the pillows, looking so fragile it was all he could do not to gather her into his arms. "I didn't mean to snarl," he apologized. "Plans for the Tour de Merrisand are well in hand. Your staff can handle anything that comes up for the next few days." Until he spoke, he hadn't thought that far ahead, but now he knew nothing was going to stop him spending the time with her and Jeffrey.

"I do feel rather tired."

He took Jeffrey's hand and urged the child off the bed. "Come on. Your mother needs a nap. Let's see if we can track down that computer game."

Jeffrey leaned over and planted a sloppy kiss on Kirsten's cheek, making Rowe wish he could do the same. In time, he thought. He had a few words with Dr. Pascale before taking the little boy to the state apartments.

Kirsten was tired, yet couldn't fall sleep. Thanks to the medication, her headache had receded, and seeing Jeffrey had lifted her spirits. So why did she feel so unsettled?

Something important had happened on the island, but what? Her brow furrowed with the effort to remember. There was the helicopter flight, the magnificent sunset, a visit to Rowe's cabana for a light meal before they decided to go for a swim. Then everything was a blur. According to Rowe, they'd been talking, then she'd gone into the water and hit her head.

Was he telling her everything? In her mind she saw herself running across a rock-strewn shore. But why? If only she could recall what they'd talked about, she might have a clue.

A sigh slipped out. Trying to remember only made the headache worse. She would concentrate on getting out of here, then ask Rowe to fill in the gaps. She owed him a lot, first for pulling her out of the surf and now for taking care of Jeffrey.

She pushed herself upright in bed, gripping the edge of the mattress until the room stopped spinning. The pain medication must be muddling her thoughts. How could she have allowed him to take Jeffrey home with him? The longer they were together, the more risk there was that Rowe would guess their real relationship. Seeing them in the hospital room, the resemblance had been almost overwhelming. He was bound to notice it sooner or later.

She swung her legs over the side of the bed. She had to get Jeffrey away before Rowe started asking questions she couldn't answer.

"What the devil do you think you're doing?" With a speed that belied his years, the doctor reached her side and eased her back into bed.

"I have to get up. My son—"

"Is safely in Viscount Aragon's care."

Her breath came out in a ragged sob. "You don't understand."

He frowned. "I may be an old country doctor, but I understand a lot more than you think."

Fear shredded her voice. "You can't possibly. Rowe doesn't."

Pascale's gaze gentled. "I'm afraid he does. The resemblance between him and Jeffrey is too strong. When you get out of here, you and the viscount have a lot to sort out."

She stirred restlessly. "When will that be?"

"Two days if you argue. Cooperate and I may discharge you this afternoon."

She had to get out of here as soon as she could. If Rowe already suspected the truth about Jeffrey… She closed her eyes, then opened them again. "I'll be a model patient from now on."

The doctor looked unconvinced, but he didn't know how much incentive he'd just given her.

Chapter Eleven

Kirsten had visited the state apartments on a number of occasions, but had never stayed in the lavish accommodation. Although the building was a century old, the apartments had been updated to include every modern amenity. Walled gardens allowed royal visitors to relax away from the public eye.

Relaxing on a chaise longue in one of the sunny gardens, Kirsten marveled at how green and tranquil her surroundings were. It was easy to forget that the busy life of the castle continued only a few hundred yards away. She could easily convince herself that she was in a country estate, far from anywhere.

She still felt guilty taking it easy when there was so much work to be done, but her assistant had assured her everything was under control. She was left with nothing to do except sip the cool drink a servant had brought for her and listen to the birds.

And worry about Rowe and Jeffrey.

In the two days since the doctor released her from

the infirmary, she could swear Rowe had been making
an effort to get closer to the child. Try as she might
to tell herself she was imagining it, he had spent far
more time with Jeffrey than at his office. He refused
to let servants take the little boy to or from school,
insisting on doing it himself. And several times she
had caught him looking at Jeffrey with a kind of
stunned pleasure, as if he couldn't quite believe the
child was real.

A chill shook her as if someone had poured ice
water over her. Was the doctor right? Had Rowe
started to question his relationship to Jeffrey before
the accident? The doctor had hinted that Rowe knew
something, but that would mean Dr. Pascale also suspected Jeffrey's paternity. She'd been a fool to think
she could bring Jeffrey to the castle without arousing
suspicion. Had some part of her wanted the truth to
come out?

Before she could explore the possibility, a childish
cry of delight tore the air and Rowe appeared in the
garden carrying Jeffrey on his shoulders.

"Look, Mommy, I'm the king of the castle," Jeffrey sang.

She laughed in spite of herself. "So I see."

"Down you come." Rowe set Jeffrey on his feet.

The child enveloped Kirsten in a sticky hug.
"What have you been eating?" she asked, sniffing
chocolate.

Rowe looked abashed. "There was an ice-cream
vendor on Parade Hill, so we had some on the walk
home from school."

Parade Hill wasn't on the way home from the Castle School. She debated whether to chide Rowe for
ruining her son's appetite before dinner, then decided

ice cream wouldn't hurt now and again. Both males looked so guiltily pleased with themselves that she smiled and said nothing.

Jeffrey leaned over the wall of the fishpond and began to watch the fish while Rowe dropped into the chaise beside Kirsten. "How was your afternoon?"

She stretched languidly. "Lazy."

"Good. Dr. Pascale will be pleased."

"He seems to know you very well," she said.

"You mean he takes liberties. After ministering to the royal family all these years, he feels entitled. Trouble is, he's usually right and he knows it."

Watching Jeffrey kick his feet against the stone wall of the pond, she struggled to find words. "He seems to think you're...attached to Jeffrey."

Rowe's gaze flickered to the little boy. When he looked at her again, the raw emotion in his expression was more revealing than anything he could have said. *He knows,* she thought, her heart sinking. *Somehow, he knows.*

"Why shouldn't I think that?"

The question was voiced so softly that she wasn't sure she'd heard him until she saw the fire in his eyes. "Did I tell you before the accident? Is that why I keep seeing glimpses of myself running away along a beach?"

"We were a heartbeat away from making love. From what you said, it wasn't hard to work out for myself that it was your first time. When I asked you, you as good as confessed that you were a virgin, and went sprinting off across the sand."

Her cheeks blazed and she couldn't bring herself to look at him. "Oh, no."

"Yet you have a six-year-old child." He leaned

across and took both her hands in his. "I nearly went crazy trying to make the pieces fit, but I finally managed it. Who is Jeffrey's mother?"

She glanced again at Jeffrey, but he was engrossed in fishing with a stick in the pond. "My sister, Natalie."

"Does Jeffrey know?"

"Yes, although I'm not sure how much he understands. I'm the only mother he can remember."

He nodded as if her answer wasn't surprising. "Jeffrey insisted on bringing a picture of you and another woman—your sister—with him to the apartment. Her features have haunted me for days, and now I know why she looks so familiar. We met at a time in my life that was difficult for me, but I'm sure her surname wasn't Bond."

Jeffrey had skipped to the far side of the courtyard to play with a life-size chess set. "She gave a false name when she crashed the party where you met," Kirsten said quietly. "Afterward she felt too embarrassed to admit that she'd lied to you."

His hands clenched and unclenched. "It wasn't the only thing she lied about. She assured me she was on the pill. Was that why she didn't want to tell me she was pregnant with my child?"

Resentment welled up inside her. "She tried to contact you by phone and letter, but she never heard back from you."

The color drained from his face. "I never received any messages from her, I swear."

He sounded so vehement she felt confused. "She called and asked for you to get in touch with her. When she heard nothing, she wrote you a letter. Still she heard nothing. It looked as if you didn't care."

His mouth twisted. "At the time I had an over-zealous manager." He dropped his head into his hands. "When I asked about messages, he dismissed them as the usual from the groupies—his words, not mine. He also took care of my fan mail. I didn't find out until much later how much he was keeping from me, and then I ended his contract. If I hadn't been under terrible pressure, I would have pressed him for details a lot sooner."

"Naturally," she said, unable to disguise her bitterness.

He lifted his head, his gaze burning. "There was nothing natural about that time. It was the anniversary of my father's disappearance and the media insisted on raking over every detail, every crazy rumor and sighting. I felt like I was being flayed alive, but I had to keep going. Too many people depended on me." His voice dropped to a murmur. "Natalie was the only bright moment in that terrible time. She seemed to understand how I felt. Neither of us meant anything to happen, but she seemed to need me as much as I needed her."

Kirsten felt her eyes tear up. It was hard to understand and hard not to feel hurt that Natalie had turned to Rowe for comfort, instead of her own sister. "We'd lost our parents not long before. She acted strong, but inside she was a wounded eighteen-year-old."

He nodded. "I was twenty-two and had already won my first world championship. Yet it only took a few bloodhounds from the media to get under my skin. When we met, Natalie and I were both hurting in different ways."

Kirsten didn't want to feel compassion for him.

Didn't want to hear that he wasn't the heartless villain she'd imagined. Yet she remembered all too clearly the stories about his father's disappearance and the persistent rumors that he was alive somewhere, hiding out. What would that do to his family, to Rowe?

"It must have been hard," she said.

"Then you believe me when I say I had no idea that I had fathered Natalie's child?"

Before she could answer, Jeffrey abandoned the chess set and launched himself at Kirsten. "There are eleventeen fish in the pond. Why are your eyes all red?"

She gathered the shreds of her composure with an effort. "I must have been sitting in the sun too long."

Jeffrey tugged on her hand. "Come inside, then. Rowe put a new Doom Planet on the computer. You don't turn into jelly. You get slimed with icky green slime."

She pulled in a deep breath. "Sounds wonderful."

Rowe stood up and held out his hand. "I'll come with you, son. Your mother needs a few minutes to herself."

Over his shoulder, he said, "We'll finish this later."

Kirsten had no idea how she got through the rest of the evening. In a few short minutes Rowe had demolished all her preconceptions about him as Jeffrey's father. If it was true that he hadn't received any of Natalie's messages, what did it mean for their future? Would he want to make up for lost time?

Fear made her start to shake. Would he want to take Jeffrey away from her?

Somehow she kept up a cheerful facade as she

coaxed Jeffrey away from the computer to eat his dinner, then played with him until bedtime. After she'd tucked him in, her footsteps dragged as she walked out of the bedroom, leaving the door slightly ajar. She loved Jeffrey more than life itself. How could she bear it if Rowe decided that his son belonged with him?

Her thoughts were interrupted by a soft knocking on her apartment door. When she opened the door, Rowe walked into the salon. Noting the partly open bedroom door, he gestured toward the terrace. The evening was fine with a gentle breeze blowing, but she barely noticed as she followed him outside.

Champagne nestled in an ice bucket on a side table. Two glasses waited beside it. The servant who had brought them said Rowe had ordered them sent to her room. "This is hardly a celebration," she said around the tightness in her throat. The doctor had told her she could have a small amount of wine if she wanted, but it was the last thing she felt like right now.

He went to the table and opened the wine expertly. "Perhaps not for you. It isn't every day a man finds out he's a father."

More afraid than she had ever been in her life, she asked, "How long have you suspected?"

He poured the sparkling liquid into the crystal flutes. "I didn't at first. I saw the resemblance right away, and I felt the bond between Jeffrey and me, but I assumed I was projecting my own needs onto him."

"I'm not sure what you mean."

"I had decided I was never going to marry and have a family," he said. "The women I'd known seemed to care more about my title than about me,

so it was easier to settle for physical relationships than
to hope for anything more.''

She accepted the glass he handed to her, although
she didn't drink, having little she wanted to drink to
right now. "I gather you didn't stop hoping."

He took a thoughtful sip of champagne. "I thought
I had. Then when I met Jeffrey, I realized I was kid-
ding myself. He's so loving and giving that he demolished the wall I'd built around my emotions.''

She drank to give herself time to think. "He has a
way of doing that. All children do."

"I don't know many children. Maybe I didn't want
to. After all, what do I know about being a father?"

He was doing remarkably well with her son, she
thought. Instinct was more powerful than he allowed
for. "Because you lost your own father so young?"

His fingers tightened around the delicate stem of
the glass until she expected it to shatter. "When he
left, I thought my world had come to an end. I even
wondered if I'd done something to drive him away."

"Jeffrey thought the same thing," she said, her
voice thickening. "He asked me if his real mommy
didn't love him enough to want to stay with him."

Rowe stared into his glass. "What did you tell
him?"

Her voice swam with tears. "I told him his mommy
loved him more than anything in the world, but God
needed her with him, so she asked me to take care of
her baby."

He released a heavy breath. "I would have given
a lot to have someone say that to me after my father
disappeared."

"Surely your mother…"

"She was too distraught herself. The servants tried

to shield me from the rumors and conspiracy theories doing the rounds, but I overheard people gossiping and started to believe that my father had started a new life somewhere else. I imagined him having a new family and forgetting about me.''

''Thank goodness we grow up,'' she breathed.

''Yes.'' His terse answer suggested it hadn't helped all that much. He may have stopped believing the rumors, but his tone said he had never stopped missing his father or wondering what had happened to him.

''What about the rest of your family?'' he asked. ''Didn't they support you and your sister when Jeffrey was born?''

''We didn't have any other family,'' she said hollowly. ''Even when my parents were alive, Natalie and I pretty well parented ourselves.''

''How did your parents die?''

She found herself wanting to tell him. Through Jeffrey, he was part of their family. ''My father was a painter, although not a financially successful one. Maybe he would have been one day. He certainly believed it, and he made us believe it, too. Something about him was enormously attractive to women, and he couldn't resist them. My mother loved him, anyway. She'd do anything for him.''

''Go on.''

''He wanted my mother to drive him to a gallery to enter a painting in a competition before it closed. There was a terrible storm and she didn't want to go out, but he was so enthusiastic that he got his way, as usual.'' Her voice broke.

Rowe lifted the glass from her shaking grasp and enclosed her hand in his. ''I can guess the rest. You were left to look after yourself and your sister when you weren't much more than a child yourself.''

"I was not a child—I was twenty,'' she said stoutly, trying to ignore the warmth coursing through her from his touch. "I didn't mind putting my plans on hold for Natalie. I knew it was only a postponement.''

"Are you sure?''

When his fingers twined with hers, she wasn't sure of anything. He had already admitted he was only interested in physical relationships, and that wasn't what she wanted. The reminder didn't stop the blood pumping furiously through her veins, sending her pulse into a frantic tattoo she was afraid he would notice.

He wasn't the man for her, no matter how much he attracted her, which she had to admit was a great deal. More than was good for her. It had been easier to resist him when she believed he had abandoned her sister and child. Now that she knew he hadn't, she had few defenses left.

Easier? The denial almost sprang from her lips. Nothing about dealing with Rowe had been easy from the moment he'd come into her life. Hard to believe it was such a short time ago that she still thought she had cause to hate him.

It certainly hadn't given her the strength to resist when he took her in his arms on his private island. Instead, she had given herself up to his embrace, and her own inexperience had betrayed her and Jeffrey.

"What else could I have done?'' she asked, not sure if the question referred to her decision to look after Natalie or her response to Rowe himself.

"You could have followed your dream,'' he said

softly. "I can't believe your only goal in life is to be an art curator, worthy profession though it is."

She shook her head, feeling unaccountably shy. Hardly anybody knew she had dreamed of becoming a writer but had put the dream on hold when she needed to make a living for herself and Natalie, and now Jeffrey. "I did want to write once," she confessed. "I know it's foolish, but..."

He touched a finger to her lips, silencing her. "No dream is foolish. I wanted to be the fastest driver on the planet, and I succeeded. Then I decided to start a business that would manage some of the biggest events in the world."

His light touch sent a shudder through her. "At least your dreams were grounded in reality." Not like her notion of writing books that would endure long after her lifetime. That dream was as fanciful as the ones that had driven her father, for all the good they had done him.

Rowe's mouth lifted into a rueful smile. "You think so? You should have heard my family's reaction when they heard I wanted to drive Formula One cars. Royalty simply doesn't do that kind of thing." When she couldn't stop herself from smiling back, he added, "That reaction had nothing on their response when I went into business for myself."

Trying not to make her need to withdraw too obvious, she moved to the stone parapet and rested her palms on the cool surface, taking deep breaths to calm the turmoil his touch always sparked within her. "They must be eating their words now that yours is one of the world's most successful companies."

He moved to stand beside her, not touching her. She trembled as if he had. "Don't bet on it. My mother still holds up my cousin, Prince Maxim, to me as an example of how a royal is *supposed* to behave. Do you still write?''

His question threw her so much she answered truthfully. "Sometimes, after I've put Jeffrey to bed." Before the accident she had been halfway through a novel centered on the art world, although she had no idea if it had any merit or not.

"Will you let me read your work one day?"

"Perhaps." To her surprise she found she wanted him to see it. She had injected part of herself into the novel. Having him read it would be like sharing herself with him.

"Will you let me be a father to Jeffrey?"

She couldn't restrain an indrawn breath of shock. Had he drawn her out, made her talk about herself and her dreams as a kind of softening-up process? "Isn't it a bit late for that?"

"I've told you why I didn't respond to Natalie's call and letter. I'm not going to beg you to believe me."

"Oddly enough, I do believe you." Even though it meant changing the thinking of years.

He seemed to sense her ambivalence. "But you still see me as an uncaring monster who would use a girl like Natalie and then abandon her."

Again her expression betrayed her. The wounded look she saw on his face in response was like a knife to her heart. "It isn't like that." How could she explain to him her fear of getting involved with him on any level, when she already had so little resistance where he was concerned?

"Then tell me what it is like."

His clipped tone was another knife thrust. "I don't want Jeffrey to get hurt," she said desperately.

"And you think I would hurt him?" More ice, crystalizing the pain between them.

"I'm sure you wouldn't do so intentionally." When it came to relationships, he was no different from her father. He would mean well, but he would end up hurting her and Jeffrey all the same. She wasn't prepared to go through that again.

"Then you leave me little choice."

Her fingers gripped the parapet so tightly that the stone left an imprint on her palms. He was going to take her child from her. As Jeffrey's father and a member of the royal family, he had the power. She would fight him of course, but she knew she stood little chance of winning.

"Look at me, Kirsten."

When she remained frozen in place, he turned her to face him, tilting her chin so she couldn't avoid meeting his gaze. His dark eyes shone with purpose. She was fairly sure she knew what it was and set herself to meet his gaze without flinching. "I won't let you take Jeffrey from me without a fight. He may be your son in fact, but he's mine by every right of motherhood there is. I raised him, I love him, and I won't let anyone come between us."

"I don't intend to," he surprised her by saying. "There's a connecting door between our apartments. Tonight I'm going to unlock it, and it stays unlocked. I had hoped you would involve me in Jeffrey's life of your own accord, but since you insist on casting me as the villain, you leave me no choice but to claim my right of fatherhood, with or without your consent."

His audacity took her breath away. Even more disturbing was the thought of the door between them standing open night and day. "I'll take Jeffrey back to our cottage," she vowed.

His gaze narrowed. "I'll simply have the servants return your possessions here until you get the message."

Could she accept his condition without risking her heart? She didn't have it in her to fight him on this. "It seems I have little option," she said.

He nodded his satisfaction. "I had to grow up without a father. There's no way I'll allow my own son to go through what I did."

What about her feelings? she wanted to demand. On the island she had almost let him make love to her. What would happen when he became part of her life on a daily basis?

He was already part of her life, she accepted on an inner sigh. Unlocking a door wouldn't change that. If she wasn't to become more deeply involved with him, it was more important to keep her heart locked against him, and she wasn't at all certain he didn't already have the key.

Chapter Twelve

Rowe was as good as his word. He allowed her the privacy of her bedroom suite, but the connecting door between them remained open. Lately he was spending more time in her and Jeffrey's salon than in his own.

Goodness knew what the servants thought of the arrangement. They were too discreet to show their feelings, although she was sure tongues were wagging. She wasn't concerned on her own account, but if any of the gossip reached Jeffrey, she would take him away from the castle and let Rowe do his worst.

What that might be, she shuddered to think. He'd said he wouldn't try to take her child away from her, but what if it happened in spite of his best intentions? She was well aware of the bond growing between father and son. Rowe may not have had a role model for fatherhood, but he had taken to the role of parent more quickly than Kirsten herself.

Nobody was born to be a parent, her mother had said often enough. You learned through being one.

Kirsten had discovered the truth of this after Natalie died when the responsibility of caring for a baby had terrified her. Somehow she had managed, growing in confidence day by day. She had forgotten those early struggles until she saw Rowe going through the same process, and his progress impressed her in spite of herself.

He impressed her on many levels, she accepted unwillingly. Cleared by the doctor to return to work after a week of rest, she had expected things to be awkward, but hadn't counted on Rowe's single-mindedness. He seemed able to compartmentalize his life into the personal and the professional far better than she could.

Maybe it was a royal skill, or at least a male one. Kirsten wished she had it. But as she worked with Rowe, she was distracted by too many things that had nothing to do with business. The way his dark hair glinted in the sunlight. The way he gestured when making a point. She wondered if he knew how expressive his body was.

The longing to touch and taste him was almost overwhelming.

According to Rowe, she had nearly succumbed to him once, on the island. Although she still couldn't remember the moment consciously, some part of her did remember, making her want to respond to him as she must have that night. It took an effort of will to concentrate on the job at hand.

The plans for the Tour de Merrisand were going well. Most of the world's leading cyclists had agreed to participate. She was feeling more comfortable about Rowe's choice of venue. As he'd predicted, the bidding for television rights was hotly contested. The idea of holding a major sporting event against such a picturesque backdrop as the castle had caught the imagination of the world's television moguls, who were falling all over themselves to broadcast the event.

The success of the race would ensure that the Merrisand Trust would have little concern about funds for many years to come. Visitor numbers to the castle were also likely to increase as a result of the favorable exposure.

A few days after returning to the office, she heard from her boss, Lea Landon. The European tour of the Carramer treasures was nearing its end, and Lea would return home within a few weeks. Freed of the burden of doing Lea's job as well as her own, Kirsten could consider her options for the first time since Rowe had come into her life. She had assumed she would go on as she was, probably succeeding Lea one day. He had made her question if it was what she really wanted to do.

She wanted to write. She knew that now. After Rowe pressed her to reveal her dream, she'd had Shara collect her unfinished manuscript from the cottage and had worked on it during her recovery. To her surprise, it wasn't as bad as she'd feared. She might even take some of her accrued leave and finish the book, then see what happened.

It would be a way to distract herself when Rowe returned to his home in Solano. A sense of desolation swept over her as she imagined the castle without his dynamic presence. She knew he wanted to keep in close contact with Jeffrey, but it wouldn't be the same as looking up to see him come through the connecting door, eager to spend time with his son.

She was going to miss him.

She looked up from the schedule she was working on to stare out the window in consternation. When had she gone from tolerating his presence to feeling lost at the idea of his going?

When had she started to fall in love with him?

Stunned, she rested her chin on her hands. It must have happened during the blank moments in her memory before she had the accident, because it felt like a truth she'd always known but hadn't acknowledged until now. Surely she couldn't be so stupid! He was everything she didn't want in a man.

And everything she did.

How on earth did one resolve such a conflict? Maybe it was better if he left, then she might be able to resolve the confusion roiling inside her. Confusion that hadn't been there until he showed up. Yes, better if he did go. She couldn't make herself believe it.

It was Shara's turn to collect Jeffrey from school today. Rowe had wanted to change the arrangement and collect his son himself. Kirsten argued that it had been justified while she was recovering, but couldn't go on without telling her neighbor the reason, one they weren't yet ready to make public.

He was even more insistent on accompanying Kirsten when it was her turn. She wasn't sure it was much of an improvement, as she was well aware of the heads turning and the murmured comments when he was with her. She was torn between pride at having him beside her and frustration at the havoc he was causing in her life.

Jeffrey had no such difficulty. He ran to Rowe with an enthusiasm he'd once reserved for Kirsten, sharing his day's activities in six-year-old language that Rowe seemed to understand perfectly.

Today, as was their habit, Shara would take Jeffrey home with her and he would play with his friend, Michael, until Shara brought him home at dinnertime. That left only her and Rowe.

He had left the office early and Kirsten could hear his voice through the connecting door when she returned to the apartment. She tensed, hearing a woman's silvery laughter in response. In the weeks they'd worked together, this was the first time he'd entertained a woman. It was to be expected of course. He was a man of powerful needs, so she shouldn't be surprised. What did surprise her was the strength of her own hostility toward the unknown woman.

Through the open door, Rowe saw her come in. "Kirsten, come and join us."

So he could flaunt his conquest? She almost slammed the door in anger, but that would be far too revealing, so she pasted a polite smile on her face and ventured into his salon.

The other woman was stunning. Seated, she was as tall as Rowe, with a figure Kirsten could tell was lithe even under the loosely draping dress. Her hair was a mass of tumbling golden curls to her shoulders, and her exquisitely made-up features were so familiar that Kirsten racked her brains for a name, but none came. She was too aware of the woman's hand tightly clasped in Rowe's.

He stood up. The woman beside him uncoiled with the grace of a cat. "Kirsten, I'd like you to meet an old friend, Tanya Hoffman."

Of course. The supermodel who reputedly commanded thousands of dollars an hour in fees. "I thought your face looked familiar,'' Kirsten said, mastering her distress enough to shake the offered hand. "I must have at least six magazines with you on the cover."

The lovely woman smiled self-deprecatingly. "It's nice being the flavor of the month. I'm making the most of it while it lasts."

Kirsten found it hard to imagine someone as lovely as Tanya being a fad, and said so. The model inclined her head. "The fashion world is fickle. Next year the editors could be falling all over some gaunt creature with no hair and a nose ring."

Rowe laughed. "I'd like to see you with a nose ring."

"You never know your luck."

Kirsten bristled with jealousy at the easy way Rowe related to the model. How close were they? The feeling persisted as Tanya asked about Kirsten's work at the castle. Kirsten couldn't have said what she replied, but it must have made sense because the other woman looked interested.

"The art world has always fascinated me. You're lucky to be working in a field you obviously enjoy."

"Don't you enjoy modeling?"

The other woman shrugged. "It's a very good living. I didn't have any idea what to do with my life until I was approached by a scout for a modeling agency. After that my future was more or less taken out of my hands. I'm not complaining, but sometimes I wonder what else I could have done."

"Well, now you're going to find out," Rowe interjected. To Kirsten he added, "Tanya is giving up modeling soon."

Was that why she was here with Rowe? The model

had been linked with Rowe by the media, Kirsten remembered. While he was still racing, photos of them together had been splashed all over the magazines and they had been filmed together often enough for wedding bells to be mooted.

Kirsten was clenching her hands together so tightly her nails bit into her palms. Was Rowe about to tell her he intended to marry the other woman? How could he when Kirsten was in love with him?

She had to face facts. She wasn't *falling* in love with him. She'd fallen well and truly almost from the moment she met him. Realizing this fact had taken her a while longer. Now the thought of his marrying someone else made her world tremble.

"Are you okay?" Rowe asked. "You've gone quite pale." To Tanya he said, "A bit over a week ago, Kirsten suffered a concussion. From the look of things, she isn't fully recovered yet."

Kirsten waved away his concern. Whatever their news, she would not break down now. Later, when she was alone, would be time enough. "I'm fine, really. You were saying you intend to leave modeling, Tanya?"

Color heated the other woman's cheeks. "Yes. My partner, Tony Margate, and I are going to have a baby."

"Tony was my chief engineer when I was still racing," Rowe supplied. "I remember the day I introduced the two of you. He looked as if he'd been pole-axed."

"He still does," she said with a laugh. "The idea of being a father thrills him, but he's also terrified."

"But you're happy together?"

"Blissfully, thanks to you, Rowe." She leaned toward Kirsten. "Tony and I had both gone through relationships where too much publicity had spoiled everything. We wanted to keep our relationship private for as long as possible, so Rowe covered for us by pretending *we* had a thing going. We fooled just about everybody."

Including her, Kirsten thought, relief making her knees weak. He wasn't involved with Tanya, after all.

Even as exhilaration flooded her, she felt ashamed of her earlier suspicions. How many of his other so-called flings were media inventions? He had tried to tell her that his playboy image was just that, an image. After her experience with her father, she hadn't been ready to trust him. Yet she could feel herself starting to. Wanting to.

"How did you keep your real relationship out of the spotlight after Rowe left racing?" she wanted to know.

"The paparazzi moved on to some other target. It doesn't usually take long." She giggled. "Rowe and I talked about staging a hugely public breakup just to get them going. Pity we didn't—it would have been fun."

"It was better this way. They left you and Tony alone for longer."

"True." She splayed long fingers over her still-taut stomach. "Now there's the baby coming. That's why I'm here. Tony's in Australia at the moment, or he'd ask you himself. We want you to be the godfather, Rowe."

Rowe beamed. "I'd be delighted. Tell Tony I accept with pleasure."

Kirsten wondered what the headline writers would make of this, but Rowe looked as if he didn't care.

Tanya looked equally unconcerned, too caught up in the wonder of her new life.

"This calls for champagne."

Tanya shook her head in negation. "I'll take a rain check until after the baby comes."

"Not for me, either," Kirsten said. "Shara will be bringing Jeffrey back in a few minutes. He's my son," she added for Tanya's benefit.

"I wonder how it will feel to say that," Tanya mused. "My son. My daughter. We haven't let the doctor tell us which we're having, and I don't really care as long as the baby is healthy. How old is your child?"

"Six," Kirsten supplied. She wondered if Rowe would say anything, but he didn't. They had agreed he wouldn't acknowledge Jeffrey publicly as his son until they had broken the news to the little boy and informed the other members of the royal family. Not sure how Jeffrey would respond, she'd begged Rowe to wait a little longer. Listening to Tanya, she wondered if she was asking too much of Rowe. He'd already waited six years, after all.

She read the awareness on Rowe's face and love for him swelled through her like a symphony. How could she ever have doubted her feelings for him? Even before she knew his so-called affairs were mostly media fiction, she'd felt the chemistry between them. Was that true love? When you cared for someone no matter what?

Tanya picked up her purse. "I have to go. I ran away from an assignment not far from here, but I really should get back. I have to be ready to start shooting a fashion spread at sunrise tomorrow at Angel Falls."

"I'm glad you managed to stop by. Let me know how everything goes, and when you need me for god-father duty."

"We will." The model shook Kirsten's hand, then stepped back and looked from her to Rowe, then to the open connecting door. "Is there any chance that you two…"

Before Kirsten could think how to respond, Rowe said, "You know what we tell the media. No comment."

"Which usually means there is some truth to the rumor. If it's true, I couldn't be more delighted for you both." She smiled at Kirsten. "Rowe is a very special man. When he loves, he loves with his whole heart. Nobody knows that better than Tony and me."

Rowe looked embarrassed, but Kirsten nodded her understanding. "I hope everything goes well for you with the baby."

"Come to the christening with Rowe. We'd love to have you."

How could she accept when the only contact she expected to have with Rowe after he left Merrisand was because of Jeffrey? The idea that he might have someone else in his life by the time Tanya's baby was born brought a lump to Kirsten's throat. "It's kind of you, but…"

"Your little boy will be welcome, too," Tanya said, misunderstanding her hesitation.

Rowe placed a hand on Kirsten's shoulder. The casual intimacy of the gesture was almost too much. "First, you have to take care of yourself and this baby, Tanya, then you can worry about the guest list."

Tanya toyed with her bag's plaited leather-and-gold

shoulder strap. "Tony won't let me do anything else. I told him I can keep working for months yet, but he's adamant this should be my last assignment."

"Quite right, too," Rowe said with a frown.

Catching Kirsten's eye, Tanya shot her a look that said, *Men!* "If you and Rowe find yourselves in our position, don't let him bully you the way Tony does me."

The other woman sounded more glowing than downtrodden. "I won't." It was easy to say, given that Kirsten was unlikely ever to have that kind of relationship with Rowe.

Hearing movement at the door to her own apartment, she said goodbye and went back through the connecting door, leaving Rowe to see Tanya out. When she let Shara and Jeffrey in, he kept up an excited chatter about the games he'd played with Michael until Shara left.

"Sounds like you had a good time, sweetheart."

His head bobbed in agreement. "Can I go and tell Rowe?"

"Not right now. He's busy with a visitor."

"Who?" Jeffrey wanted to know.

She stroked his silky hair, as black and glossy as Rowe's. "None of your business, little snoops. Why don't you get into your pajamas and I'll ring for your dinner?"

At his bedroom door, Jeffrey stopped short. "How come you don't cook stuff anymore?"

"I will when we go home to our cottage."

"When?"

She went cold. Kneeling beside him, she asked, "I thought you liked living here."

"Yes, but not for always. Why can't we live in a

proper house? You can be the mommy, and you could get me a daddy like Michael's."

Her heart threatened to stop. "Daddies aren't easy to find, sweetheart."

The little boy tilted his head to one side. "Rowe can be my daddy."

"Would you like that, Jeffrey?"

At the sound of Rowe's voice, her head jerked around. He was standing in the open doorway, his expression taut. Don't do this, she beseeched him silently. It's too soon. "Jeffrey was just going to get ready for supper."

The child's mouth set in a line she knew from experience meant trouble. "I don't want supper. Michael's mommy gave us waffles. I want a daddy."

"Not everybody has a daddy these days," she said desperately. Why did Rowe have to come in now and fuel a dangerous discussion her child wasn't ready for? "What about Jimmy and Helen?" They were twins in Jeffrey's class, and Kirsten knew that their mother was raising them alone. She could think of a number of children in a similar position.

"Jimmy and Helen have a puppy."

Her hopes rose as she saw a possible way out of her dilemma. "Maybe we can think about getting you a puppy. Would you like that?"

"A big shaggy black one?"

She wished she wasn't so conscious of Rowe hovering nearby, waiting to see where the discussion would lead. "How about a small shaggy black one?"

Jeffrey thought for a moment, then shook his head. "Nah, I really want a daddy. He can play ball with me and give me pony rides and play Doom Planet. Rowe can play Doom Planet real good."

"Really well," she said automatically. "Why don't you go to your room and draw me a picture of the puppy you'd like to have?"

The child's face brightened. "Can I draw a picture of Rowe?"

The potential subject's shoulders shook, but he kept a straight face. "Why don't you draw both?"

Jeffrey's grin widened. "Rowe *and* a puppy. Wow." He spun around and almost ran into his bedroom.

"Don't slam the—"

Crash.

"—door."

She got to her feet, finding she was trembling. Without asking, Rowe poured iced water for her from a crystal decanter. When she took the glass and drank from it, the ice rattled. "Looks like I'm going to have to get him a dog."

Rowe's intense gaze bored into her. "Why not a daddy? You have to tell him the truth sometime."

She cradled the glass in both hands. "We talked about that. He isn't ready."

His eyebrows arrowed into a frown. "He sounded ready enough to me."

"You don't know him as well as I do."

"And that's the problem, isn't it? You don't want me to, do you."

She looked around wildly, but there was nowhere to go. "Of course I do."

"Provided I keep my distance and play the role of kindly uncle. He's my son, Kirsten. I had to live without my own father most of my life. I know what it was like. I won't do the same to Jeffrey just to protect your cozy one-on-one relationship."

Putting the glass down, she regarded him bleakly. "This isn't about me. It's about what's best for my child."

His savage gesture dismissed her argument. "Your child, your son. Isn't it time you stopped seeing him as an extension of yourself? He's a person in his own right. You heard him—he wants a father."

"He's heard other children talking. He's too young to understand what he's really saying."

"Then explain it in words he can understand. Tell him about me. Tell him I would have been there for him all along if only I'd known he existed. Tell him how much I regret the time we've lost, the time I can never give him back." His eyes were filming and his hands were balled into fists at his sides. His voice was hoarse. "Tell him that his daddy loves him and his mother very much."

He spun around and walked through the connecting door. Distantly she heard his apartment door closing behind him.

She stared after him in amazement. Had she heard him correctly? Did he mean he had loved Natalie? Slowly it dawned on her that he had said "loves," present tense. She cupped her hands to her face, too stunned even for tears. He couldn't mean that he loved her, Kirsten, could he? He must have meant to include her only as Jeffrey's mother. Heaven knew, she should be grateful enough for that.

She closed her eyes. Anything else was too astounding to contemplate.

A loud sniffle made her open her eyes. Jeffrey stood beside her in his pajamas, the buttons crookedly fastened. He was struggling to hold back tears. She reached for him, adjusting the buttons with icy fingers. "What's the matter, sweetheart?"

"You made Rowe go away."

A cold hand closed around her heart. How much had he heard and understood? "He hasn't gone away. He had...he had something he needed to do."

A gulping sob greeted this. "No, he didn't. You made him mad. Now he doesn't wanna be my daddy."

How could she answer that? "We did have a little argument, sweetheart. It doesn't mean he can't be your daddy if it's what you want."

Jeffrey nodded, dashing tears away with a closed fist. "I want you and Rowe to be my really, truly mommy and daddy together."

Her despairing sigh ruffled his hair. "I'm afraid that might not be so easy."

"Why not?"

She'd been asking herself the same thing. Rowe's parting words had made her wonder if there was a chance for them, after all. She was surprised how much she wanted it. "It's a long story."

Hearing the magic word, *story,* Jeffrey's face brightened. "Tell me, please?"

It was time, she saw. She patted the sofa beside her. "Jump up here and get comfy. This could take a while."

Chapter Thirteen

With Jeffrey snuggled into the crook of her arm, she began to tell him a story about a small boy just his age who wanted a father. He had a real father of course, but his daddy didn't know about him. His daddy lived in a castle far, far away.

"Like Merr'sand?" Jeffrey asked.

"Just like Merrisand."

"And the little boy is six and his name is Jeffrey."

Her mouth curved in a smile, although she felt as fragile as glass. "His name is Jeffrey, and he had a beautiful young mother called Natalie."

By the time she finished the story, tears were pricking her eyes. "So you see, you have a real mommy in heaven, a mommy who lives with you and takes care of you, and a real daddy who lives in another place. We all love you very, very much."

Jeffrey squirmed in her grasp. "Can I visit the 'nuther place where my daddy lives?"

"He would like that a lot."

"Can I live there?"

Oh, no, please, she prayed silently, staring her greatest fear full in the face. "Do you want to?" she asked, hardly daring to breathe.

Jeffrey's hand curled into hers, sending slivers of pleasure through her. "Only if you come, too."

"That's the hard part," she explained gently. "Sometimes your daddy will want you to visit without me so he can have you all to himself. I'll always be waiting here when you get home."

The child's mouth set in the familiar stubborn line. "Not going, then."

"I thought you were happy that Rowe is your daddy."

Jeffrey rested his head against her side, making burrowing movements. Love for him wound tendrils around her heart, almost choking her. "Why can't we be in the same house? Michael's mommy and daddy are in the same house."

Blinking hard, she kissed the top of his head. "Michael is a very lucky boy."

"I'm a lucky boy."

"I know you are, sweetheart. Luck comes in different ways. You and I are lucky to have each other."

He reached up and gave her a wet kiss, saying sleepily, "I love you, Mommy."

"Love you, too. As much as all the world and all the sky." She took refuge in the phrase she had used to comfort the little boy for as long as both could remember. Tomorrow was soon enough to decide how she and Rowe would share Jeffrey's time. Tonight he was still her baby. She swung him up into her arms and blew a raspberry against his cheek. "It's way past your bedtime."

He laughed, then yawned hugely. "I'm not tired."

"So I see. Bedtime, anyway."

He protested sleepily as she tucked him in, but his heavy lids had closed before she turned on the night-light he still liked to use. Her gaze fell on the photograph of her and Natalie that Jeffrey had insisted on bringing to the apartment. Natalie looked heart-breakingly young to have borne a child and left the world without having the chance to see how well he'd turned out.

"'Night, Nat," Kirsten said under her breath. She glanced at the sleeping child. "You can be proud of Jeffrey. Tonight must have been hard for him to understand, but he really tried. Now that he knows he has a daddy, I only pray I don't lose him to Rowe."

Her voice broke and she fled from Jeffrey's room, half closing the door carefully behind her. She had known this time would come, but had hoped her baby would be older before he asked about his father. She hadn't counted on Rowe himself being part of their lives when the moment came.

Where was he now? She knew better than to think he had turned to another woman. More likely he had gone to the office to work. Or maybe to stare at the wall the way she was doing, wondering how this could be resolved without anyone getting hurt.

Somebody was bound to, she knew, and she pressed her palms tightly together, promising herself it wouldn't be Jeffrey. However carefully they tried to prepare him to spend time with them both, he was bound to be unsettled by the experience. It seemed inevitable that he would choose between them one day. And she had seen how closely he bonded with Rowe. They were father and son. It was only right.

Except that it felt as if she stood on the edge of a precipice while stormy waves eroded the land beneath her feet.

Nothing had been decided yet, she reminded herself. She might well be on the brink of losing her child, but it hadn't happened yet. Perhaps Jeffrey would adjust happily to living some of the time with her and the rest with Rowe. She believed in miracles. She had to believe in this one.

Needing the solace of activity, she reached for her laptop computer and opened her files on the Voyager exhibition coming up at the galleries. By the time the exhibition opened, the Tour de Merrisand would be over and Rowe would be gone, she thought. The list of possible exhibits blurred before her eyes.

What would he say if she told him she loved him? He would probably think she was only saying it to retain her hold on Jeffrey. Rowe had already accused her of wanting to keep her relationship with her child exclusive. He wouldn't put it past her to pretend affection she didn't feel in order to get what she wanted.

He was wrong about her attitude toward Jeffrey. She wanted to protect the child, not take over his life. She had never wanted that. If Natalie had lived, Kirsten would happily have played the part of doting aunt. If Rowe himself had chosen his staff better, he would have known about his son a lot sooner, she thought angrily. He was as much to blame as she was for the years lost between him and his son.

She began to type furiously, taking her annoyance out on the keyboard. More than an hour had passed by the time she pushed the hair back from her face and regarded her handiwork with satisfaction. Anger had its uses. By chaneling it into her work, she had chosen exhibits she could weave into a narrative thread that would hold any visitor's interest. Lea would be pleased when she got back.

Time to look in on Jeffrey. Closing the computer, Kirsten stood up and stretched, then froze as she noticed the child's door standing wide open. She was sure she'd only partially closed it when she'd come out. Ice water ran through her veins as she moved to the door, already fearing what she would find.

His bed was empty.

She pressed a hand to the sheets. They were cold. How long had he been gone? She must have been so deeply engrossed in her work that she didn't hear him slip past her. A check of Jeffrey's closet revealed that his school jacket and bag were missing. Dread clutched at her like a dead hand. Rowe's apartment was also empty.

Outside both apartments, the long corridors were deserted, the ponderous ancestral portraits staring down at her in mute accusation. She ran back inside and dialed Rowe's office, having to start again twice because her fingers shook so badly.

Be there. Be there. Be there. "Aragon."

How could one word lift her spirits so? "Rowe, it's Kirsten. Is Jeffrey with you?"

"No. Is something wrong?"

"He's missing. I...I told him about you tonight before tucking him into bed. And now he's not there! I thought he might have run to you."

"Or away from me."

"Never that. He loves the idea of having you for a daddy, but he wants us to be together. I think he's upset because I told him it wasn't possible."

She heard Rowe's sharply indrawn breath before

he said, "I'll have the guards check the grounds. You go to the cottage in case he went there. Take your phone with you so we can keep in touch."

She grabbed her cell phone and headed for the cottage. It was in darkness and showed no sign of the little boy. Her neighbors hadn't seen him, either, but volunteered to help search. At this time of night the castle was closed to visitors and the gates were guarded, but a small boy could slip through a gap in a hedge, be anywhere. She was achingly aware that Angel River crossed the castle boundary not far away. Sharing her fear, Paul and Shara said they would check along the river.

When her cell phone rang she almost jumped out of her skin. It was Rowe. "Meet me at the Castle School. I've got an idea."

His torch bobbed toward her as she came within sight of the school's wrought-iron gates. Usually flung wide in welcome, they were closed and the grounds were dark. At the base of a gatepost, she spied a small huddled figure and flew to it, heart pounding. "Jeffrey?"

Clad in his school jacket over rumpled pajamas, he looked frail and vulnerable as she gathered him into her arms. "Sweetheart, what are you doing here?"

"Waiting for you and my daddy to come and get me."

Her heart leaped into her throat. The only time Jeffrey could rely on them being together was when they picked him up from school. She looked up at Rowe, leaning over them. "How did you guess?"

"When you said he wanted us to be together." Handing her the torch, he lifted the sleepy child, the small head drooping against his shoulder. "Let's get you home to bed, son."

While they walked, she called the others to end the search. At the apartment anxious servants waited to help, but she insisted on putting Jeffrey back to bed herself, watching over him until she was sure he was asleep.

"This time I've locked the outer doors of both apartments," Rowe whispered.

She hadn't heard him come in. "He's never run away before."

"He's never had to deal with a situation like this before."

That made two of them, she thought as she followed Rowe quietly out of the bedroom. And she wasn't six years old. Her extra years didn't seem to help.

A brandy decanter and two glasses were set out in the living room. "I thought you might need a nightcap. I know I do."

She watched him pour the drinks and took hers, but didn't taste it. Her thoughts were already chaotic. Alcohol wouldn't improve matters. He sat down on the sofa beside her, not touching her. Her body vibrated as if he had. "At the office, I did a lot of thinking. Jeffrey's right, we should be together."

For the sake of the children. How often had she heard her parents use those exact words as reasons to stay together. Stay together and torture each other. "If we're careful, he'll get used to the idea of parents who live apart. Lots of children do."

"They're not my son."

Her heart skipped a beat. "Are you saying you want permanent custody of him?"

He lifted the glass from her fingers and cupped her hands in his. "I'm saying I want us to be together. I meant what I said before, Kirsten. I love Jeffrey *and* his mother."

His touch felt electrifying. "I thought you only wanted a physical relationship."

His gaze caught and held hers. "I thought so, too, until you came into my life." His expression lightened. "I've no doubt ours will be as physical a relationship as you can have. That night on the beach showed me how wonderful it would feel to hold you in my arms. I want to make love to you so much it hurts."

Flickers of memory surfaced, so potent she couldn't catch her breath. She remembered his kisses and her awkwardness betraying her virginal state to him. She must have run away from him then, but she still couldn't remember that part, or falling and hitting her head. All she remembered was being held in his arms. She wanted it now more than she wanted air to breathe. Still, she needed to know, "Are you saying these things only because of Jeffrey?"

"Does this answer your question?"

He pulled her into his arms until she felt the fast beating of his heart keeping time with her own. His mouth found hers and she clung to him, answering his hunger with her own desperate longings. Deeper and deeper. Thoughts whirling. Body clamoring. Yes, they could share this. So easy to surrender when every part of her urged it. And yet...

Feeling her grow tense, he lifted his head and regarded her questioningly. "What is it?"

She dragged the words out. So hard, so hard. "You've shown me in many ways how good we can be together physically. But there has to be more—for me, anyway.''

"For me, too.'' He released her and began to pace. "For years I never knew whether I was loved for myself, my title, or my sporting celebrity. Nobody got close to the core of me—until you. Natalie was there for me in my dark night of the soul, but we wouldn't have lasted. She was too young, too irresponsible.''

He swung around, his eyes glittering. "Then there was you. I told myself we could have an affair and it would be wonderful. No need for anything more lasting. Except…you'd gotten under my skin. The night you were injured, I couldn't stand knowing I had caused you pain. It was then I knew I was in love with you.'' He looked rueful. "Maybe there is some truth to the legend that says anyone who serves the Merrisand Trust will be rewarded by finding true love. I know I have.''

He dropped to his knees beside her. "You must know by now that I'm a different man from your father.''

"I've known it for some time,'' she said in a voice barely above a whisper. Kirsten had come to know Rowe as a man of great passion, but also great loyalty. Not the kind to take love lightly, no matter what the media said about him.

"While I was in the infirmary, I had time to think about my father. I recalled something I'd almost forgotten.'' Or hadn't wanted to face, she thought. "Before he and my mother went out into the storm, I heard him tell her he loved her. He said he hadn't always been a good husband, but he promised he would change. He never got the chance.''

Rowe stroked her hair. "The main thing is, he was

willing. Your mother must have loved him a great
deal to stick with him through thick and thin. It isn't
hard to understand when you feel the same way yourself.''

She nodded, feeling her eyes brim. She'd thought
she knew what love was, but she hadn't even come
close until Rowe. Now she understood what her
mother must have known always, that true love didn't
come with conditions. You either loved or you didn't.
No middle ground.

None with Rowe, anyway. The desperate racing of
her heart sounded in her ears and her breathing was
ragged. ''How do you know so much?''

He took her hands, kissing her open palms. ''I
don't, and I'm starting to think nobody really does.
All we can do is try. Are you willing to give our
relationship a try, Kirsten?''

She pulled her hands free and brought his head
against her breast. Desire, so poignant it was close to
pain, raged through her. Joy filled her in a dizzying
rush. ''Who am I to argue with a legend?''

He straightened, raining kisses along her arms.
''We'll get married right away.''

Her laughter bubbled up. Guiltily she glanced at
Jeffrey's bedroom door, but he hadn't stirred. ''Even
you can't arrange a royal wedding overnight.''

His hands were busy on the fastening of her dress,
easing it off her shoulders so he could trail his lips
along her collarbone. ''Then we'll run away together.''

Heat seared her wherever he touched. She arched
her back, aware of an urgency that threatened to con-
sume her. ''Running away isn't easy with a six-year-
old child.''

"I guess it's the wedding, then." He caressed her until she felt so aroused she wondered how she would ever be able to wait for the ceremony.

She pressed her hand against his heart. "What matters is how we feel here."

He covered her hand with his. "If you feel half what I do, the waiting will be agony."

How well she knew. "Worth it to be together for always."

He groaned, but began to put her dress to rights. "Why does everything worth having come with a price?"

How often had she asked herself the same question? "So we appreciate it all the more."

He finished with her dress and began to stroke her hair. "I don't think it's possible for me to appreciate you any more than I do now."

It seemed easier to show him how totally she agreed. She linked her arms around his neck and captured his mouth in a kiss that threatened their precarious resolution. When she came up for air, she said, "This is going to make our son very happy."

He smiled. "Our son. I like the sound of that. Of course, our daughter sounds good, too."

"But we don't have—"

He silenced her with another kiss. "Not yet, but give us time."

Still holding him tightly, she slid to the floor beside him, thrilling to the feel of his hard body against hers. "I will."

All the time in the world.

Epilogue

The seat beside Kirsten was left empty by design. She didn't care what others thought of her insistence on it, but she wanted to save a place for Natalie tonight. A symbolic place. Her sister's child was the star of this evening's performance, after all.

She was sure Natalie would approve of the way things had worked out, although she would probably be as astonished as Kirsten herself to think Kirsten had been Viscountess Aragon for two whole months now. Even after the elaborate ceremony held at Taures Cathedral and a magical honeymoon at Rowe's secluded island, Kirsten still felt as if she was dreaming. They'd given the days to their son and the nights to each other. Waking up to find him beside her every day was like a miracle.

"Happy, darling?" he asked, threading his fingers through hers.

"Nervous," she said, gripping his hand. "What if Jeffrey forgets his lines?"

She saw Rowe's mouth twitch. "Could that be the reason his teacher is standing in the wings with a prompt book?"

"But he's so young to have the lead role."

"Relax. I took part in my first Journey Day Pageant at the same age."

"Did you play the monarch?" Jeffrey had been chosen to play one of Rowe's ancestors, Prince Jacques de Ville de Marigny, the first ruler to journey around all of Carramer's islands, unifying them for the first time in their history. The voyage was commemorated annually throughout the kingdom.

Rowe shook his head. "I was the rebel chief of the last island to agree to unite under the Carramer flag. I was a method actor. I decided my people were head-hunters and attacked the prince's party, until my teacher reminded us that there have never been head-hunters in the kingdom."

Feeling better, Kirsten smiled. "What a spoil-sport."

"I'm glad you're on my side. A little dramatic license never hurts."

A rustle traveled through the audience of parents, family and friends at the arrival of Prince Maxim and Princess Giselle. Both served on the board of the Mer-risand Trust and attended events at the Castle School whenever they could.

Would she ever manage to look as impressively regal as the princess? Kirsten wondered. The rest of the audience resumed their seats and the lights dimmed.

"Looks like we arrived just in time," Maxim said to Rowe. He leaned across Rowe to Kirsten. "How's our stage mother?"

"Torn between biting her fingernails and swelling with pride," Kirsten admitted. At first she'd been in awe of her royal relatives, but they had accepted her into their family so completely that she understood why Rowe loved and respected them so much.

Sometimes she missed her work, but she was already finding she had her hands full in her new role at Rowe's side. The Tour de Merrisand had been a huge success, and the funding for the Merrisand Trust was assured. Now Rowe was helping Maxim plan for the trust's future. They had decided to remain at Merrisand Castle for the time being. Eventually they intended to find a home nearby; that way Jeffrey could continue attending the school where he was so happy.

Rowe straightened, as if to emphasize that his son was the one leading the pageant. "Here they come."

She had to admit that Jeffrey looked impressive. His costume, copied from an old woodcut of the historic journey, consisted of leather pants and a jerkin laced across his chest. Over his shoulders was a long, feathered cloak fastened by a jeweled emblem, a genuine antique Maxim lent him for the occasion.

His face set with purpose, the little boy strutted across the stage to where a group of islanders waited under a grove of papier mâché trees. "I am Prince Shark," he roared. The effect suffered a little when a whispered voice from the wings prompted, "Prince Jacques."

"I am Prince Jacques," Jeffrey repeated without missing a beat. "I bring peace to all the islands."

After that, the pageant went smoothly. "Prince Shark" was not referred to again, and by the time every child in Jeffrey's class had appeared as the islanders who had united to become modern-day Carramer, Kirsten's eyes were misting. She wasn't the only one, she saw, as cast and audience rose to sing the national anthem, "From Sea to Stars."

As their teacher ushered the children off the stage to enthusiastic applause, Rowe turned to Kirsten. "Our son may be the first member of the royal family to embrace a theatrical career."

Thinking of Prince Shark, she wasn't so sure, but basked in the glow of his fatherly pride as she followed him outside to wait for Jeffrey. "He did do well, didn't he."

"He did magnificently," Prince Maxim said, joining them. "I don't think I have ever seen a better Prince Jacques."

Rowe pretended indignation. "I don't know. As the rebel leader, I wasn't bad in my day."

"Talent obviously runs in the family," Princess Giselle said dryly. "Unfortunately, as a girl, I never got to play the prince, or I'd probably have outdone all of you."

Maxim grinned at her. "Spoken with true female modesty."

The princess's eyes sparkled. "Why must we be modest about our achievements? Haven't you heard the story that Prince Jacques was really a woman disguised as a man? Records suggest there was a Jacqueline de Ville de Marigny, and none of the official portraits show them together."

The princess kept her voice low, and they stood apart from the other audience members, watched over at a discreet distance by members of the Royal Protection Detail. Still, Maxim shifted uneasily. "My dear sister would like to rewrite all Carramer history from a female perspective. Yet no one denies there have been strong women in the royal family who've influenced our progress.''

"As consorts of the real rulers." Giselle turned to Kirsten. "Given a choice, wouldn't you rather be on the throne than the power behind it?"

"Perhaps, if I'd been born to the job." Like Giselle herself, Kirsten thought. She had the look of the warrior queen about her. Yet she served Merrisand at her brother's side, rather than in her own right. It didn't sound as if the situation pleased her.

The princess gave Maxim a fierce look. "In Carramer, being born to the job means being born male. Kirsten, you don't know how lucky you are, marrying a man with no such antiquated ideas."

Maxim looked affronted. "My ideas are not antiquated."

Giselle linked her arm through his. "Max, I love you dearly, but male chauvinism runs through your veins as predictably as your royal blood."

The prince rolled his eyes in mock despair. "Say something, Rowe. The honor of the de Marigny males is at stake."

Giselle wasn't letting up. "If I was allowed to serve the Merrisand Trust in more than a token capacity, the legend might work for me, then I would be out of your hair."

Kirsten turned in time to see Jeffrey run toward Rowe. He swung their son into the air, then, after setting him down again, held out his hand to pull her to his side. He grinned. "Maybe you should take Giselle up on that challenge, Max. It would be interesting to see what happens."

Maxim looked dubious. "You don't really believe

the legend about anyone serving the trust being rewarded with true love, do you Giselle?''

The princess gave a half smile that didn't conceal
the wistfulness behind it. ''It worked for Rowe and
Kirsten.''

''As art curator, Kirsten was serving the trust long
before Rowe came long. They would have found each
other with or without the legend,'' Maxim asserted.

Kirsten wasn't so sure. She'd been employed by
the trust, but hadn't really *served* it until she chose to
set aside her initial opposition and help Rowe to make
the Tour de Merrisand a success.

If you trusted it, the legend rewarded more than
mere work. You had to give from the heart, as Kirsten
knew she had done. Now it was up to the princess to
make the discovery for herself. First Giselle had to
find her heart's path, then follow it to where love
waited. Without doubt, a quest worthy of a princess.

* * * * *

Will the Merrisand Trust strike again?
And how far will Princess Giselle go
to win the right to head the trust—
and discover the identity
of her mysterious champion?
Find out next month in

THE PRINCESS AND THE MASKED MAN
(SR #1695)

If you enjoyed what you just read,
then we've got an offer you can't resist!

Take 2 bestselling love stories FREE!

Plus get a FREE surprise gift!

Clip this page and mail it to Silhouette Reader Service

IN U.S.A.	IN CANADA
3010 Walden Ave.	P.O. Box 609
P.O. Box 1867	Fort Erie, Ontario
Buffalo, N.Y. 14240-1867	L2A 5X3

YES! Please send me 2 free Silhouette Romance® novels and my free surprise gift. After receiving them, if I don't wish to receive anymore, I can return the shipping statement marked cancel. If I don't cancel, I will receive 6 brand-new novels every month, before they're available in stores! In the U.S.A., bill me at the bargain price of $21.34 per shipment plus 25¢ shipping and handling per book and applicable sales tax, if any*. In Canada, bill me at the bargain price of $24.68 plus 25¢ shipping and handling per book and applicable taxes**. That's the complete price and a savings of at least 10% off the cover prices—what a great deal! I understand that accepting the 2 free books and gift places me under no obligation ever to buy any books. I can always return a shipment and cancel at any time. Even if I never buy another book from Silhouette, the 2 free books and gift are mine to keep forever.

209 SDN DU9H
309 SDN DU9J

Name _____ (PLEASE PRINT)

Address _____ Apt.# _____

City _____ State/Prov. _____ Zip/Postal Code _____

* Terms and prices subject to change without notice. Sales tax applicable in N.Y.
** Canadian residents will be charged applicable provincial taxes and GST.
   All orders subject to approval. Offer limited to one per household and not valid to
   current Silhouette Romance® subscribers.
   ® are registered trademarks of Harlequin Books S.A., used under license.

SROM03   ©1998 Harlequin Enterprises Limited

Your opinion is important to us! Please take a few moments to share your thoughts with us about your experiences with Harlequin and Silhouette books. Your comments will be very useful in ensuring that we deliver books you love to read. *Please take a few minutes to complete the questionnaire, then send it to us at the address below.*

Send your completed questionnaires to:
Harlequin/Silhouette Reader Survey, P.O. Box 9046, Buffalo, NY 14269-9046

---

1. As you may know, there are many different lines under the Harlequin and Silhouette brands. Each of the lines is listed below. Please check the box that most represents your reading habit for each line.

Line	Currently read this line	Do not read this line	Not sure if I read this line
Harlequin American Romance	❏	❏	❏
Harlequin Duets	❏	❏	❏
Harlequin Romance	❏	❏	❏
Harlequin Historicals	❏	❏	❏
Harlequin Superromance	❏	❏	❏
Harlequin Intrigue	❏	❏	❏
Harlequin Presents	❏	❏	❏
Harlequin Temptation	❏	❏	❏
Harlequin Blaze	❏	❏	❏
Silhouette Special Edition	❏	❏	❏
Silhouette Romance	❏	❏	❏
Silhouette Intimate Moments	❏	❏	❏
Silhouette Desire	❏	❏	❏

2. Which of the following best describes why you bought *this book?* One answer only, please.

the picture on the cover	❏	the title	❏
the author	❏	the line is one I read often	❏
part of a miniseries	❏	saw an ad in another book	❏
saw an ad in a magazine/newsletter	❏	a friend told me about it	❏
I borrowed/was given this book	❏	other: _____	❏

3. Where did you buy *this book?* One answer only, please.

at Barnes & Noble	❏	at a grocery store	❏
at Waldenbooks	❏	at a drugstore	❏
at Borders	❏	on eHarlequin.com Web site	❏
at another bookstore	❏	from another Web site	❏
at Wal-Mart	❏	Harlequin/Silhouette Reader	❏
at Target	❏	Service/through the mail	
at Kmart	❏	used books from anywhere	❏
at another department store or mass merchandiser	❏	I borrowed/was given this book	❏

4. On average, how many Harlequin and Silhouette books do you buy at one time?

I buy _____ books at one time	❏
I rarely buy a book	❏

MRQ403SR-1A

5. How many times per month do you shop for any *Harlequin and/or Silhouette* books? One answer only, please.

1 or more times a week	❑	a few times per year	❑
1 to 3 times per month	❑	less often than once a year	❑
1 to 2 times every 3 months	❑	never	❑

6. When you think of your ideal heroine, which *one* statement describes her the best? One answer only, please.

She's a woman who is strong-willed	❑	She's a desirable woman	❑
She's a woman who is needed by others	❑	She's a powerful woman	❑
She's a woman who is taken care of	❑	She's a passionate woman	❑
She's an adventurous woman	❑	She's a sensitive woman	❑

7. The following statements describe types or genres of books that you may be interested in reading. Pick *up to 2 types* of books that you are most interested in.

I like to read about truly romantic relationships ❑
I like to read stories that are sexy romances ❑
I like to read romantic comedies ❑
I like to read a romantic mystery/suspense ❑
I like to read about romantic adventures ❑
I like to read romance stories that involve family ❑
I like to read about a romance in times or places that I have never seen ❑
Other: _____ ❑

The following questions help us to group your answers with those readers who are similar to you. Your answers will remain confidential.

8. Please record your year of birth below.

   19 ____

9. What is your marital status?

   single ❑   married ❑   common-law ❑   widowed ❑
   divorced/separated ❑

10. Do you have children 18 years of age or younger currently living at home?

    yes ❑   no ❑

11. Which of the following best describes your employment status?

    employed full-time or part-time ❑   homemaker ❑   student ❑
    retired ❑   unemployed ❑

12. Do you have access to the Internet from either home or work?

    yes ❑   no ❑

13. Have you ever visited eHarlequin.com?

    yes ❑   no ❑

14. What state do you live in?

    _____

15. Are you a member of Harlequin/Silhouette Reader Service?

    yes ❑   Account # _____   no ❑   MRQ403SR-1B

COMING NEXT MONTH

#1694 FILL-IN FIANCÉE—DeAnna Talcott
Marrying the Boss's Daughter

Recruiting well-mannered beauty Sunny Robbins to pose as his bride-to-be was the perfect solution to Lord Breton Hamilton's biggest problem—his matchmaking parents! Sunny wasn't the titled English aristocrat they expected, but she was a more enticing alternative than *their* choices. And the way she sent his pulse racing… Was Brett's fill-in fiancée destined to become his lawfully—*lovingly*—wedded wife?

#1695 THE PRINCESS & THE MASKED MAN— Valerie Parv
The Carramer Trust

Beautiful royals didn't propose marriages of convenience! Yet that's exactly what Princess Giselle de Marigny did when she discovered Bryce Laws's true identity. Since the widowed single father wanted a mother for his young daughter, he agreed to the plan. But Giselle's kisses stirred deeper feelings, and Bryce realized she might become keeper of his heart!

#1696 TO WED A SHEIK—Teresa Southwick
Desert Brides

Crown Prince Kamal Hassan promised never to succumb to the weakness of love, but Ali Matlock, his sexy new employee, was tempting him beyond all limits. The headstrong American had made it clear an office fling was out of the question. But for Kamal, so was giving up Ali. Would he trade his playboy lifestyle for a lifetime of happiness?

#1697 WEST TEXAS BRIDE—Madeline Baker

City girl Carly Kirkwood had about as much business on a Texas ranch as she did falling for rancher Zane Roan Eagle— none! Still, she couldn't deny her attraction to the handsome cowboy or the sparks that flew between them. Would she be able to leave the big city behind for Zane? And could she forgive him when the secrets of his past were revealed?

SRCNM1003